A BEARD PARADOX

A BEARD PARADOX
BY LAWRENCE SCHIMEL

Translated into English by Sandra Kingery

Art by Stefano Cipollari

REBEL SATORI PRESS
New Orleans & New York

First published in Spanish in 2016 by *Una barba para dos* by Lawrence Schimel.
Copyright © 2016 Lawrence Schimel.
English Translation copyright © 2024 by Sandra Kingery.
This edition © 2024 by Rebel Satori Press.

Cover and interior images by Stefano Cipollari.

Rebel Satori Press
www.rebelsatoripress.com

Designed by Nieves Guerra.
ISBN-13: 978-1-60864-305-9

Library of Cogress Control Number: 2024938466

TABLE OF CONTENTS

INTRODUCTION

Lawrence Schimel

A Beard Paradox is my fourth published collection of short stories, but it also represents a number of firsts.

It is my first collection of microfiction, in which I set out to explore whether the erotic—which to me depends so much more on context and the dynamics between characters than the hydraulic or mechanical details of sex—could be expressed within the compressed format of flash fiction. Each story is a maximum of 500 words, or both sides of a single sheet of paper.

It is also the first work of adult fiction that I wrote directly in Spanish, what I often jokingly refer to as my "stepmother tongue," having lived now in Madrid, Spain for over two decades. While my last two collections were published in Spanish before being published in English, those books were originally written in English—even if while living here—with Spanish translations commissioned by the original Spanish publisher.

There was a gap of around 15 years between publishing collections three and four, during which I wrote and published many books for younger readers and also worked extensively as a literary translator, both into English and increasingly into Spanish as well.

A Beard Paradox is not the first time I have been translated into English, my mother tongue, although it is still a fascinating, illuminating experience each time. It's been a joy to see these stories take on a new life in Sandra Kingery's translations and to watch her come up with solutions, especially for word play or double entendres, that would never have occurred to me.

Tony Kushner once wrote "It is impossible to write about sex and not reveal too much of yourself. Whereas I think it is possible to have sex and reveal nothing of yourself whatsoever."

I've discovered a new layer of what has been revealed to me about myself in seeing these stories translated into English by someone else—and how they take on a different life in English as a result. It's been a kind of personal maturity to step back and let someone else make her own choices and decisions in how to interpret and transpose my stories between languages and cultures that I also share.

It has also been curious to watch how the act of translation (by someone else) has also granted these stories—despite their intensely sexual content—a patina of respectability as they've been published in journals and anthologies (and now in book form): they are literature in translation, that just happens to be about sex. (If they'd been written in English or self-translated I imagine they'd likely be considered just smut.)

With 100 different stories, this collection is like a box of chocolates: tiny bursts of different flavors you only discover when you bite into them. I hope these erotic morsels delight and excite as they now find new readers in English.

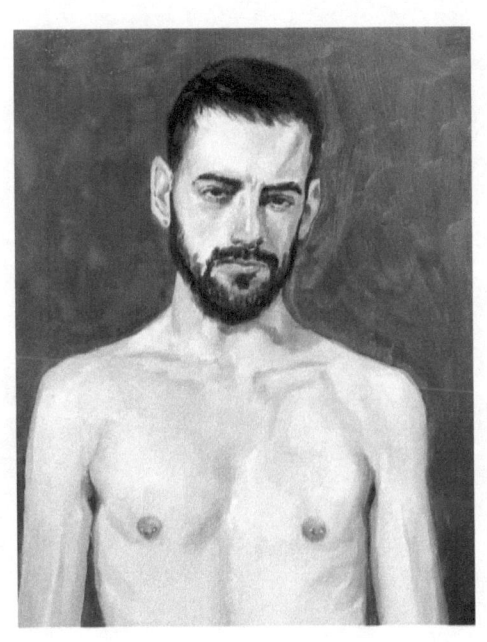

PRECARIOUSNESS

Given the price of condoms, we decided to close the relationship. At least until one of us finds a job.

BUZZ CUT

I complained to a friend that ever since I shaved my head, only bottoms hit on me. When I see him again, his head is shaved as well. And for the first time, I find him attractive.

"I listened to you," he says.

"It works," I reply. I place my hand on his thigh.

He smiles at me and moves my hand—repositioning it onto his crotch.

CAT-SITTER

You have to jiggle the key until you find the sweet spot, but I finally manage to open the door. One of the cats is waiting for me right on the other side of the landing, but when it sees that it's me and not my friend, their owner, it turns around and disappears into the apartment. I go inside and close the door, setting my things on the hallway table.

I feel strange, as if I were doing something illicit.

I pour more dry food into their bowl, give them fresh water, clean the litterbox that's in the bathroom.

My friend asked me to give them some TLC as well—this is the part that makes me feel weird. I sit on her bed, imagining they'll come. I assume it'll take a while. While I wait, I look around the room. There's a basket of dirty clothes, and on top, there's a pair of boxer shorts. They're her boyfriend's. She went to Palencia with him, they're spending Semana Santa with his parents. The cats don't come. I stand up and go over to the basket. I take the boxers and bring them to my nose: yes, they still smell like him. That pleasant scent of the sweet sweat of his balls.

My dick's hard. I inhale again, touching myself.

When I open my eyes, the cats are standing there, watching me.

Good thing they can't tell my friend.

GRAFTED

What people always want to know is where we all go when it comes to sleeping.

Most of them imagine the three of us together in one big bed, taking turns penetrating or being penetrated, or that one of us is lucky enough to be in the middle penetrating and being penetrated at the same time, or two penetrating the third simultaneously. They divide our roles according to their own fantasies, what they dream about doing or having done to them.

Some people think that the couple still sleeps together and I sleep in some broom closet by the kitchen, like a servant, except when I'm taking care of their needs (sexual or otherwise) like a male geisha.

Or just the opposite, other people imagine the original couple, with strong bonds of affection between them but no excitement anymore, sleeping in separate bedrooms like in a black and white Hollywood movie from the '50s, and that I'm the solution to avoid their breakup, satisfying one or both of them with my youthful virility.

What's hardest for almost everyone is imagining our life outside of bed. A three-way domesticity. Take my hand and try to imagine it. You too, take my other hand. That's it. Let's close our eyes now and imagine together. A life for three, no matter how we met or in what order. Imagine an absence of jealousy. Supporting each other. Celebrating one another. So much power together. So much love.

A CRY PIERCED THE NIGHT

It was after one in the morning on a weeknight, and I was kneeling down in a vestibule sucking off a neighbor. We didn't know each other, but I couldn't sleep, so I went on Grindr, which was perfect for those times when proximity was more important than almost any other factor. I won the lottery that night, because the guy lived very close by, and he had a nice meaty dick. He was waiting for me at the door, one hand inside his sweatpants, touching himself. We didn't leave the entryway but I didn't care. I could just make out his boner and it made my mouth water. We didn't say anything but everything had already been said before I arrived. I went to my knees and revealed his succulent cock, I took it in one hand, squeezing it, stretching it until the foreskin slipped aside and revealed the head. I opened my mouth and was in ecstasy for a few minutes, jacking myself off while I blew him, immersed in that pure sex zone where you're not thinking about anything else, you forget the stress of daily life, only pleasure, absolute and simple, enjoying what I was doing, without wanting anything else to be done to or requested of me.

Suddenly, a cry pierced the night.

By the time I realized it was the wailing of a baby, my mouth was empty. The neighbor had left, closing the door to the rest of the house behind him.

Did he do it so I wouldn't go in looking for him or so the people on the other side wouldn't see me?

Was there a jealous wife behind that door who would get mad if she caught him?

Or maybe it was a gay couple with a kid, anything's possible nowadays.

I went soft thinking about the different scenarios.

My knees hurt.

In the heat of the moment, I hadn't realized it, but now, after cooling down, I felt ridiculous, kneeling there, alone, without knowing what was going to happen. I thought about jacking off, coming, and heading home, leaving a stain on the floor.

But I could have stayed home for that.

The crying finally stopped.

I licked my lips. I could still taste him, and I knew I wasn't going to be satisfied until I could finish giving head—to him or some other guy—, but the idea of starting to look again, at that time of night, felt like way too much work, not to mention the uncertainty. It was late enough that I couldn't be sure I'd get any.

The possibility of being caught made me even more excited.

I stayed there, on my knees.

I stretched my neck, rocked back on my heels.

Finally, the door opened.

I felt my heart sink into the pit of my stomach: was it him or his partner?

He was back. He was holding a baby that was sucking on a bottle.

He hadn't doubted that I'd still be there, waiting for him, waiting for his cock.

"I've got something for you to nurse on as well."

I lowered his sweatpants and began.

AFTERWARDS

He asked if he could shower before leaving.

Then he got dressed and left, with a last kiss and a "thank you," polite but nothing more.

On the one hand I was pleased, because I didn't feel like sleeping with anyone that night, especially not a stranger. But the sex hadn't been bad and I wouldn't have minded seeing him again. I didn't say anything to him either. But it was a blow to my self-esteem. Even if I hadn't wanted to see him again, I wanted him to want it.

I went into the bathroom to pee before going to bed.

I started laughing as I flushed: he'd written his phone number in the condensation on the door to the shower.

POETRY RECITAL

"Virgin Mother of all that's holy! I think I just discovered religion and that guy is its one true God. Have you ever seen such beauty made flesh?"

Hugo turned his head to look.

"You mean Salva?"

"You know that exemplar of masculinity?"

"I even know him Biblically."

"Now I know you're pulling my leg. He looks like a porn star."

"I don't know if he's ever made a flick. He's a gogo dancer at Space."

"And you've really fucked him? How much did it cost?"

"He's not a hustler, or at least he wasn't with me. It lasted a few weeks. He's with Luis Antonio now."

"What's the deal? He's got a poet fetish?"

"No, just the opposite. He wants to be the poets' fetish."

"You're fucking kidding me."

"I'm serious. He's hot and he knows it. But since taking your clothes off every night in a disco is so ... ephemeral, he wants to be immortalized in verse."

"I'll write him some iambic pentameters right now, singing praise to the muscles in those legs ..."

"You're going about it all wrong. The secret with Salva is to be distant. Let him conquer you. Make him work at driving you crazy."

"I don't know if I'd be capable of not surrendering at his feet if he deigned to talk to me ..."

"Well, you've got time to work on your self-control. He hasn't been with Luis Antonio very long, he'll want to be his muse a few more weeks. Salva doesn't like poetry, but he knows that no one can predict who's going to succeed in the world of letters. He wants to go down in posterity, so he's decided to try all the poets. It might not last long, but while he's with you, it's incredible. You'll see. Read some sexy poem tonight but don't show him much interest. Sooner or later, it'll be your turn."

THE CRACK OF DAWN

His alarm rang and I got up. He's a zombie in the morning, capable of putting salt in his coffee instead of sugar (he's done it), so I went to the kitchen to turn on the coffeepot and put sugar in his cup, leaving everything ready for him for when he got out of the shower.

I cover my eyes when I go into the bathroom, not to avoid seeing him naked but so the light doesn't wake me. I take a piss and go back to the bedroom, closing the door behind me. Two minutes have gone by and the bed still holds his heat. I curl up in the hollow his body left in the sheets, hugging his pillow. Breathing deeply, everything smells like him and I start to get hard. What a dilemma now: masturbate or go back to sleep?

SECOND THOUGHTS

I was showering before leaving when he appeared and got under the showerhead next to mine. I hadn't seen him earlier, when I was circling the hallways in search of something worthwhile. I had ended up having a forgettable lay with some guy in one of the rooms, he was the best of what I saw during a few rounds. But it had only been a physical effort (it took me a bit of work and imagination to get into it) and in the end a little water was enough to erase any trace of the encounter from my body and my memory.

But I sure would have enjoyed myself with this hottie if I'd seen him sooner!

His body was slender, the skin so white that I could almost make out the blue veins flowing underneath it. Skin that would show off the red marks from my hand, as if framing every blow ...

I didn't know if he had just arrived, or if he'd been busy in some cubicle and that's why I didn't see him when I was prowling around. In any case, I took pleasure in watching him caress himself under the streams of water, washing his short black hair, but more than anything rubbing his body with the lathered gel.

There were a few showers free, so his decision to use the one next to mine wasn't a coincidence. I love it when a guy knows what he wants and has no reservations about going after it. I admired him openly and it was obvious that my interest was growing.

Even though he was clean, the boy started soaping up again, this time looking at me over his shoulder, while his hands and the gel disappeared between the smooth white cheeks of his ass.

The invitation was clear, and I decided I didn't need to leave so early, my body ready for a second round.

I extended my hand until it reached one of the perfect globes of his ass.

He smiled at me, so I took a step forward and joined him under his shower.

RESULTS

I got super hard when the doctor told us: "All negative." I used to wonder sometimes whether he still remembered screwing that other guy, which led to those three months of sex with a latex barrier between us. But it didn't matter anymore. Now I wonder if we have to wait to get home or if he'll let me blow him in the bathroom of some bar on the way, until I can savor the taste of his pleasure again.

BLINDFOLDED

It not only intensified my other senses, but gave me a new one: being an object of desire.

When he ran his hand down my back, shoulder, thigh, I not only felt him, I imagined how he was seeing me: solid but submissive, all his.

My stiff cock danced on its own, calling out for attention, waving at anyone who was looking at us there in front of the open window.

MACHOS IN THE METRO

I'm always aware of who's around me in the metro. For two reasons. One is that I like to snap pics of hot guys without them realizing. I pretend to be texting or browsing Facebook, but I'm actually capturing portraits of raw masculinity: an unshaven square jaw, a bulge at the crotch of some sweatpants, the biceps of a guy holding onto the pole when the car starts to slow down. And it's an even bigger turn on because they're not aware of my admiration and idolatry.

The other reason is that I often open Manhunt while I'm traveling, refreshing the screen at every stop to see the faces (and often the dicks) of the guys that the GPS detects nearby. And even though I'm in favor of reclaiming public spaces for displays of affection between gay couples, two guys kissing or holding hands is one thing and a screen, even though small, with erect schlongs is another. The truth is that when we're out in public, we all stick our noses into what other people are doing around us—just take a look at my archive of hotties, as one example.

I also recognize that looking at sexual profiles in a supposedly inno-cent context, like on the metro, adds a thrill of the forbidden; it reminds me of how furtive hooking up with someone in person used to be in the pre-smartphone era, when it all started with glances, a smile, perhaps some accidental contact, to indicate intentions and test the waters.

And it gets complicated at every stop because of the flood of people entering and exiting, like a living Tetris, with those of us who remain on board shuffling ourselves into the empty spaces before the invasion of new bodies.

Pulling into a station, I had Manhunt open, hiding the screen with my body so no one else could see it. During that dance of adjustment, I ended up nearly pressed up against this really amazing hunk, an absolute colos-sus whose very presence made my knees weak and my mouth water. I wanted to take a picture so I could remember him better at home ... But we were squished in like sardines, my shoulder and arm pressing against the hard plate of his torso and his six-pack abs, and there wasn't enough distance to capture more than a tiny detail at point-blank range.

So I just inhaled his imposing presence, looking at him out of the corner of my eye in that forced intimacy, until we reached the next station, where the train stopped abruptly and, since I wasn't close to a pole, I didn't have anything to hold onto and I started to fall.

But the guy grabbed onto me by the hand that was holding my phone.

And for one instant, we were frozen there, as if his immense strength had stopped time, and there was nothing more than that contact of my wrist in his hand, the feel of skin against skin while he looked into my eyes in a fixed and indecipherable fashion. I felt delicate while also feeling bathed in the intense aura of his masculinity.

Then the door opened and, without letting go of my arm, he turned his head to see the screen, which showed the dick pics on some guy's Manhunt profile.

NEW CONSTELLATIONS

"It's incredible," said Pep, lying on the grass looking up at the sky, "we never see this many stars in Barcelona."

I'd rented a farmhouse for the weekend with some friends, who in turn brought other friends who I met there for the first time. Pep was a friend of my friend Lluís, but I still wasn't sure whether they were more than friends.

We'd had a type of picnic dinner out on the field behind the house, and now we were finishing the bottles of wine and enjoying being so close to nature and so far from the city and our urban lives.

"I think that's the Ursa Major," said Lluís.

Antonio stood up, clutching his belly. "No, that's me, I'm the Great Bear," he said.

We all laughed, and started telling jokes. We were somewhat tipsy and enjoying the good mood that comes from being outside and not having any obligations for a whole weekend. It was one of those moments that sometimes develops between people who share something, something that later turns into a type of personal vocabulary, private and shared among them.

We started shouting out new erotic constellations, a whole celestial Kamasutra.

"The dildo."

"The Prince Albert."

"The fisting."

Between jokes and laughter, I had rolled down a small incline and I suddenly realized that Pep was by my side and that we were alone there, on that green strip beneath the sky.

There was a long moment of silence, in which I couldn't hear the rest of the group, so close and simultaneously so far, a moment in which Pep looked at me.

"The kiss," he said, his voice so low that only I could hear his whisper.

"The kiss," I repeated, tilting my head toward him, our breath inter-mingling, our lips finding each other.

I closed my eyes and we kissed, and with my eyelids still closed, I saw the stars.

DEMOCRATIC

They were both very ugly. I wouldn't want either of them to touch me. I asked myself how much they'd have to pay me before I'd consider the possibility of having sex with either one of them. But I couldn't help it, my eyes turned to them over and over again to watch while one kneeled down in front of the other. Against my volition, blood rushed to my crotch, my dick stood up as if it also wanted to look at them with its blind eye, one of their cocks disappearing into the mouth of the other and vice versa.

"It's too democratic," complains my best friend about the showers at the gym. He always showers at home after working out with me.

THE CHOICE

When I walked by, the men lowered their pants.

One of them had such a huge cock that it didn't get completely hard.

One had a normal one.

Another had two cocks, both the same, like mirror images.

Another had huge balls, like grapefruits, which made his dick look small in comparison.

One took my head in his hands and kissed me, first with his tongue, then our lips just barely touching.

I followed this last one home.

OUTDOOR CAFÉ

"The problem with these tables," I insisted "is that it's impossible to pick someone up if he's sitting at a different one. Or even someone standing up, just walking by or heading to the metro. An exchange of glances, sure, that works. But getting any further, extremely difficult."

"With the whole plaza watching," said Toni, "you'd have to be pretty bold ..."

We both looked at Jairo, who was sitting with us but his attention was elsewhere. Probably on some guy. We didn't say anything, but Toni and I shared a smile, and we continued talking about other things. From time to time, Jairo added some commentary, or shared some anecdote about his experiences cruising in the park close to Ventas.

We asked for the check so we could go get something to eat. Two groups of guys showed up before the waiter did, wanting the table when it was free.

The three of us crossed the plaza, but Jairo suddenly pulled away from us. He approached a table and dropped a napkin in front of some guy, who was sitting with another guy.

"I can't believe it," I said when Jairo joined us again.

"How do you know the other guy wasn't his boyfriend?" asked Toni.

"And what if he is? But I doubt it. Didn't you see how he was looking at me the whole time we were sitting there?"

"Olé, olé," I said, impressed and also somewhat jealous. "Even though he's not going to call you, you've got the biggest balls I've ever seen."

But I was wrong. We hadn't even left the plaza when Jairo's phone rang.

"You're fucking kidding me," said Toni. "Is it him?"

Jairo didn't stop, he kept walking until he got to the corner of Gravina Street. There, in the park, out of everyone's line of sight, he finally took out his phone and read the message. He smiled.

"Tell us!"

"You can't just leave us hanging!"

"The squeaky wheel gets the grease," said Jairo with a smile. "I'll leave you here. I've got a date for a lube job."

FRESH OUT OF THE OVEN

I put my scarf on before heading out. You could just discern the first morning light through the window, marking the gradual transition from winter to spring, but it was probably still cold at that time of morning. I turned the deadbolt twice, out of habit, even though I was only going down for a minute. After so many years, my routines were established: I woke up early, even on Sundays like today, and I went down to buy bread fresh out of the oven.

I heard that *ding* that indicated the arrival of the elevator and I started to get in, still on auto-pilot, before the doors were fully open. That's how I bumped into the young guy from the apartment in front of mine, who was coming out of the elevator. He grabbed onto me and since I immediately saw that he was drunk and obviously coming home from a night out at the same time as I was starting my day, I held onto him so he wouldn't fall over.

We stayed in each other's arms so long that the door to the elevator closed.

I studied his face, so close to mine. I had seen (and heard) him before, but I'd never paid much attention to him. I was almost twenty years older, I thought, and I suddenly felt old. I remembered when I was twenty-something and would come back from the bars at this time of morning after a crazy night on the town. But I felt very distant from this skinny young dude I had in my arms, as if he were a different species: one side of his head almost completely shaved, a piercing under his lower lip, his unbuttoned jacket revealing brightly colored synthetic clothing, probably meant to shine under the ultraviolet lights of the discos.

In spite of my aversion, I couldn't remember how long it'd been since I felt another man in my arms and I didn't let go. My job no longer left me with time to look for one-night stands. Plus I didn't understand the current rules and expectations. Looking for something longer-lasting seemed like a fairy tale. Sure, same-sex marriage was legal now; I just didn't have any candidates, whether they were frogs, princes or normal men.

The automatic light in the hallway clicked off as well, leaving us in the semi-darkness of the landing.

"Sorry," I said at last, releasing him and taking a step back. "I was going down to get bread and I didn't expect there to be anyone in the elevator at this time of morning."

He flicked the light on and looked me up and down without saying a word. I imagined he was scrutinizing me with the same aversion I had felt. He might not even realize I was gay.

Or maybe that turned him on more, because he grabbed his crotch and said: "I can give you a baguette right here if you like."

He's drunk, he's a neighbor, it could get messy, I thought.

But I deviated from my morning routine and followed him to his side of the hallway. Man cannot live from bread alone. And I no longer felt so old.

PRIDE

It wasn't a question of my boss finding out I'm gay, since I'm out at work and in the rest of my life. My dilemma, when I sat up and peered past my boyfriend's back down the beach, came from seeing my boss, in a tiny phosphorescent yellow bathing suit, walking in my direction with his wife. I turned my head to the left, estimating where they were going and calculated that they'd have to pass right by me to get to the only gap between the stretched-out bodies that was big enough to extend two towels.

I examined that miniscule piece of cloth again, imagining what was underneath it. Then I looked at my own crotch, where there was absolutely nothing to leave anything to the imagination. That was my dilemma.

There are always a lot of factors that influence the decision about whether to go naked or not when you arrive at a beach: the kind of shape you're in, whether you're well-hung, who you're with, if you're looking for some action or not, etc. We'd already seen every variation around us: normal guys and Adonises, nude guys, guys in every type of bathing suit, brand-name pretty boys who took off and put on their D&G swimsuits that cost them a fortune, and guys who were like matryoshka dolls, with smaller and smaller pieces of clothing on underneath each previous one: jeans, shorts, speedos, thongs, etc.

Rafa doesn't like tan lines. I'm of the opposite opinion, I think those white shadows that emphasize an ass in contrast with the tan are very sexy. But since Rafa looks at my ass more than I do, I didn't mind giving in to him.

But I hadn't expected to run into my boss, especially with this difference in clothing. If we were both naked, or both clothed, I wouldn't be obsessing over it so much.

I had three options:

a) Turn over and pretend to be sleeping, hoping he hadn't seen me. I doubted that my boss—unlike hundreds of guys in Madrid, not to mention other cities—could recognize me by my ass alone.

b) Try to get into my swim trunks before he got there. But it would be even more humiliating if he caught me in the middle of that operation.

c) Do nothing.

I elbowed Rafa to wake him up: "That guy that's coming this direction, he's my boss."

Rafa chose a fourth option that sent a chill down my spine in spite of the sun. He stood up and said: "Well, introduce us then."

VODKA WITH LEMON SODA

I was in the kitchen, serving myself a drink, when I happened to hear part of a conversation between two guys in the hallway.

"I tried to use the bathroom but I think there were two people in there."

"It's a party," responded a voice that I knew well, the boyfriend of my co-worker Natalia, whose birthday we were celebrating. "What do you expect?"

"OK, but I think it was two guys."

"Well, you know Natalia likes gay dudes. She's one of those ... what do you call them ... a *fag hag*. That's why she has so many male friends ..."

They moved down the hallway and I couldn't hear them anymore. But I'd heard enough.

"What a hypocrite," I said out loud.

"What'd you say?" asked a voice behind me. I turned my head to look at her. It was one of Natalia's friends, we'd been at a few parties together but I didn't know her very well.

"Nothing," I answered and, raising the bottle I was holding, I asked: "Do you want a drink?"

"Thanks."

"Cheers," I said and raised the glass to my mouth, hoping that the vodka would mask my breath, after having just given Natalia's boyfriend a blow job in the bathroom.

HOLY WEEK

I hate waiting.

Someone brushes against me, but the sidewalk's so crowded that it's not worth getting upset about, and I simply push the hand away.

He insists, pushing me a little, and I pull my arm away again.

You take my hand, turning it until it's cupping your crotch.

I'm immediately as hard as you are.

"When we get home ..." you whisper in my ear, pressing your groin against me to emphasize your meaning.

I hate waiting.

I imagine lying in bed, arms and legs tied to the four corner posts, crucified and awaiting you.

Just then, we hear the procession approaching at last.

LOST CAT

There was a xeroxed sign with a photo of a cat posted all over Chueca. The third time I saw it, I stopped to read it:

MISSING
BLACK AND WHITE CAT
HIS NAME IS METEORITE
HIS OWNER IS A TOP
WITH AN 8" DICK

I searched the whole neighborhood, but there wasn't a single tear-off phone number for the cat's owner left on any of the posters.

HOT AND COLD

It's not something we put on our online profiles, but we could have. If this relationship fails at any point and I need to be on the market again, I may include it. I get cold really easily. I not only have cold feet all winter but, with the way I sweat, my skin stays cool even in summer. Nacho says that touching me in the summer is wonderful.

Even when it's 100 degrees out, I sleep covered up. It creates a kind of microclimate that I need so as not to feel cold. Nacho's the opposite. He gives off heat all year round. That's why, in the summer, he sleeps buck naked. If I get up to take a leak at night, when I come back I love to stop in the doorway for a minute, half asleep, and observe him in the blue light of the alarm clock, naked and radiant. But in the winter, it's just the opposite. It's wonderful to get between the sheets and discover they're already warm from the heat of his body. He even puts up with it when I stick my cold feet between his own, which are always toasty warm. But later on, when we fall asleep, he wraps himself in the blankets like a cocoon, keeping all his heat inside. The shock of the cold wakes me, but he sleeps like a log and there's no way to unwrap him. So I've learned to sleep with another blanket by my side, for when I find myself suddenly uncovered.

It's almost better that we didn't include this detail about one of us always being hot and the other always cold in our profiles; on paper (or on the screen), it might have seemed like one of us would quench the other to create a tepid relationship, friendly but with no spark. But the truth is that it's been just the opposite, in part because we're both very flexible in our sexual desires and appetites and that means we never get bored. We're like the yin and the yang, forming a whole that's greater than its parts. And taking turns in sharing those two forces between us.

LUNCH TIME

I always loved to try to guess what Luis was making for lunch by the smells that would hit me when I opened the door every afternoon after getting home from work.

"Something with balsamic," I said, following the olfactory clues through our apartment to the kitchen, where my boyfriend was standing at the stove. "And potatoes."

"Just in time," he greeted me, giving me a quick kiss before turning his attention back to the frying pan. He set a plate on top of it and flipped the tortilla española, with a perfectly executed maneuver, not splattering anything, the way I would have.

I turned toward the other countertop, where I found two plates ready to be served, with some greens sautéed in the balsamic vinegar reduction that I had smelled from the doorway, on a bed of baby lettuce.

"It looks straight out of a cookbook," I said, in astonishment. "You must have spent all morning cooking."

"I missed you." He hugged me from behind, kissing the back of my neck, his hands (no longer distracted by the food) holding me across the chest and then playfully traversing my torso while he rubbed his crotch against my backside.

"I can see that," I answered, laughing, and without turning around, I grabbed his ass with one hand, pulling our bodies closer.

Suddenly, my stomach began to growl, and we let go of each other, both of us laughing.

"I think my body wants to satisfy other appetites first," I said.

Luis turned off the gas and slid the tortilla onto a plate. Then he took me by the hand: "Let's go to bed."

"And lunch?"

"It'll taste just as good cold," he assured me. "I know you. You won't feel like it after eating. You'll just want a nap."

He was right. After eating, I always feel slow and sluggish, and sex feels uncomfortable, like nothing more will fit inside me, not in my mouth or in my ass, no matter how appealing it was at another time.

"Come here. This is what doesn't taste as good when it gets cold." And he lowered my hand to his crotch. My stomach let out another growl, but my dick started growing once I touched his hard-on, hot and eager, through his jeans.

"Let's go to bed," I agreed. "For the first course."

"And to work up a real appetite!"

A BEARD PARADOX

I hadn't even thought to pay attention to the clean-shaven man who was right beside him: beards are simply magnets for my eyes. Not to mention for my dick. As they were coming toward me down the sidewalk, I suddenly realized that the smooth-faced guy was watching me look at the bearded guy at his side—his partner? A friend?

I thought, at first, that he was upset.

But when our paths crossed, with the guy I found hot still unaware of my interest, and his beardless companion still staring at me fixedly, I realized that, far from being angry, he was looking at my own beard.

WRITING EXERCISE

The exercise for our fourth class was to describe a tattoo. I chose one I have on my calf, an eagle with its wings extended, describing its shape, location, when I had it done, etc. After half an hour, we had to put our pencils down even if we hadn't finished. The professor asked for volunteers to read what we'd written out loud. I felt proud of my description, but I was too shy to talk in public. That's why it was Nando who read his exercise:

Thirsty. It made me thirsty to watch the drop of sweat that was balancing at the top of the hill formed by his bicep, as if the tribal tattoo encircling his arm were holding it in place. He lowered the hand that was holding the 20-pound weight and the droplet slipped free, sliding slowly down his skin until disappearing into the valley of his elbow. I wanted to follow that path with my tongue, try to trap those salty drops, sate my thirst with them.

Our gazes met in the mirror. I was holding a 2-pound weight in each hand, standing next to him, but without exercising. I was looking at him, and he realized it. My throat was dry. I wanted to say something to him. But I couldn't think of anything to say. My mind could only formulate a single word: "Thirsty."

He was the one who broke the ice: "Nice tattoo," he said.

I'd never paid attention to him before that. It never even crossed my mind to wonder if he was gay or not. But now, I not only wanted to break my pencil and throw out what I'd written, I was dying to take him to bed. Or wherever. Because in spite of his normal, even boring, physical appearance, with that kind of imagination ... it was sure to be something worth writing about afterwards.

BOOKCRUISING

I walked out of the club, inhaling the night air deeply.

I'd had a good time, but I was tired and the truth of the matter is that discos aren't my favorite place to be. I go to hang out with friends and, of course, to possibly meet guys. Sometimes I go back to some dude's house and we have mediocre sex because we're both exhausted or the other guy's plastered ... The usual.

When I felt like I'd danced enough, I chose to leave rather than trying to hang on half the night. I could still get almost eight hours of sleep if I put earplugs in and wore a mask that I'd held onto after a transatlantic flight ...

I was already imagining being in bed when I realized someone had left a book in the doorway of a building. I bent down to get a better look at the title: *Passion* by Brane Mozetič. I'd seen some reviews of the book on a blog, but I still hadn't read it, so I picked it up off the ground.

I was wondering whether someone had lost it, or perhaps they left it on purpose, a *BookCrossing* that no other passerby had picked up yet. It was a strange place to leave a book, I thought, until I opened it and read the note stuck inside the cover: *It's hard to find a man who likes literature as much as sex. If you like both, give me a call and we can have a shag (perhaps like the one on page 39) and talk about these stories. Or why don't you suggest something to read or a position for us to try?*

AN UNEXPECTED MEETING

I really didn't realize it was him when we entered the bar. He was by himself, leaning against a wall, his left hand bound to his shoulder in a sling.

Interesting, I thought, both his injury and the guy himself, in that first fleeting impression: beard, well dressed, worthy of a second glance.

He was behind me, my friends had placed themselves along the opposite wall, and I was talking with them but wondering about that guy, how he hurt himself, how it would affect us if we hooked up.

I turned to look and it was him.

I'd been so afraid to run into him again after I'd kicked him out of the house and when I finally did, I didn't even recognize him.

"We did," my friends responded, when I confessed I hadn't realized it was him.

We stayed a while longer—us talking, him and me mutually ignoring each other—and when they'd finished their beers, my friends and I went to another bar.

I wanted to return home, not only to avoid a possible confrontation if he also remained on the prowl, but to look at Facebook: he never checked his privacy controls and his timeline was public. I wanted to find out what had happened to him without having to talk to him. I wanted to know without him knowing I knew. Knowledge was power. But I'd promised myself to stop spying on him in that way, which didn't do any good. That's why, remembering what had happened, when I got the urge to check his profile today, I turned the computer off and wrote this entry on the first page of a notebook another guy had given me as a gift years earlier.

CALCULATIONS

I had suspected that Félix wasn't wearing anything under his sweat-pants, but when he came back from the bathroom after peeing, I confirmed it and my own briefs began to feel tight. How was I going to be able to continue thinking about quadratic equations when my eye was being drawn, like iron to a magnet, by that little spot on the fabric, one of those little drops of urine that always comes out late, after shaking your dick? I didn't care about tomorrow's test, I wanted to stretch him out on the bed and lower his pants, revealing the only square root that interested me right now. I was trying to discern his shape underneath the cotton, measuring every movement by eye, but I wanted more; I wanted to feel his heat against my hand, get to know his smell of sweat, his taste. And at the same time, I was hoping that Félix wouldn't notice my desire, the non-altruistic reason I was helping him with math. I loved numbers because I knew how they would respond, it was people who remained an unknown for me. I could calculate, for example, how long his dick was now, at rest, from what I could make out, and then calculate its final extension if I stretched out my hand to place it on his crotch and squeeze it and stroke it; what I was unsure of was how Félix would react, and that's why I was still plagued by doubts over whether my calculations were correct.

JAYWALKING

The police stopped him for trying to cross the street against the light.

"But you don't understand..." he tried to explain to them, looking over his shoulder at the sidewalk on the other side of the street. His justifications fell on deaf ears. They not only stopped him, but they also gave him a fine.

When they finally released him, before he'd even stuck the ticket in his pocket, a man who was nearby and had observed everything approached him.

Now what? He didn't raise his eyes to look at him, not because of shame, but imagining that he might go away if he didn't give him any attention.

"That was so unfair," said the man who didn't go away.

"Well, you know, they probably have quotas for the number of fines they have to give out a day and all that ..."

"I would have crossed the street to follow that guy as well. What a hunk!"

Suddenly, he looked up at the guy who was talking to him, smiling at him. Nice-looking, neither handsome nor ugly, pleasant.

And they shared that desire for the guy he'd been trying to follow.

"Can I buy you a drink? It'll help you get the bad taste out of your mouth from the cops and the guy who got away ..."

He smiled in response.

That other guy was really hot, but there was almost no way he would have paid any attention to him.

While this guy ...

In the end, while they were walking toward a bar, he thought: maybe it'll be worth it to have to pay every penny of that damn fine!

THE NEITHER/NOR GENERATION

"Have you realized," said Enric, looking out at Sitges Beach, "that we're now the Neither/Nor Generation, but à la gay? We're no longer skinny, but we're not fat enough to be bears. We're not kids anymore, but we're not old enough to be daddies either. Neither one thing nor the other. We're precisely what isn't a fetish for anyone."

"Stop complaining so much, cariño," responded Alberto, standing up and shaking out his towel. "And how about we head back to the hotel and have a quickie before we meet up with Ricky and Fredo for cocktails?"

FRESH SHEETS

Even though Juanjo was still brushing his teeth, I got undressed, leaving my clothes in the basket, and climbed in between the fresh sheets on the bed. I always changed the linens on Saturdays, even when I had to work second shift, like today, so I'd changed them that morning, while Juanjo was making fruit pancakes for breakfast. I turned the washing machine on first thing so I could hang everything up to dry before I left for work. And now, after a long day, I was finally stretched out in bed.

All of a sudden, I felt something scratchy on my side. I slid over and saw a white line that was already dry; it made its way across the cotton and disappeared beneath my body.

I started getting hard as soon as I saw it. I began stroking myself slowly with one hand while I waited for my husband to come to bed and told him: "Why don't you tell me about your afternoon, mi amor."

LAST STOP BEFORE HIS DESTINATION

Turning his gaze from the window of the train, Dani looked at the woman who was sitting next to him reading the most recent book by María Dueñas. At least she was distracted, he thought, because what topics of conversation could they have in common? Sometimes he wondered how RENFE, the Spanish train company, chose who to pair up for these journeys, and he imagined how different the trips would be if people could select their own seatmates, not only by gender or physical attractiveness (some eye candy would make trips easier to endure), but by mutual interests or something like that. Luckily, his iPhone was almost fully charged and his headphones let him shut out the rest of the world. That was almost always a good thing, except at times, like now, when he didn't want to be alone with his thoughts or with the stress of feeling trapped, confined, both by his family and his hometown, even though he still hadn't made it back there yet.

The door to the compartment opened, and he looked up, seeking any distraction to avoid thinking about the long weekend that was awaiting him. To his surprise, he found that a man of around his own age was looking at him over the back of the seats while walking down the aisle. He recognized that gaze; not the guy himself, but his interest. A gaze that swiftly jumped to the face of the woman beside him and then back to him, trying to guess the relationship between them. Dani opened his mouth, as if to answer the question the other guy had not yet posed ...

But it was too late, he moved past Dani's row and continued walking toward the back of the train. Dani sought his reflection in the window, but couldn't see anything other than rolling green landscapes extending to the horizon.

He let a few minutes go by and then, apologizing to the woman sitting next to him, got up and headed toward the food car. But the man wasn't there. Dani hesitated between ordering something and waiting for him to show up or continuing his search for him throughout the rest of the train … But then he felt ridiculous and decided to go back to his seat. At least the walk, although brief, had distracted him.

But before getting back to his own car, the bathroom door opened just as he was walking in front of it. And there he was, the man he'd been looking for. They made eye contact again and remained frozen and expectant during a long pause.

Then the other guy, instead of exiting, took a step back, opening the door a little bit more as a sign of invitation.

Thinking about what was awaiting him in his hometown and how impossible it was going to be to escape that environment, Dani only hesitated for an instant before also entering the bathroom and closing the door behind him.

Now at least when he reached his destination he would be more relaxed.

TOOTHBRUSHES

He handed me a damp towel so I could clean our semen off my belly and dick. "You can stay if you feel like it," he said.

I don't usually stay after hookups with strangers. But we'd had a good time, and yes, I felt like it.

"But I need to go to sleep now," he added. "I have to get up early, at 6:30."

That was when I usually got up too, so the time didn't scare me. I was also convinced by thinking both about the pleasure of sleeping next to him and not needing to waste time going home that night.

"I'd like that," I said, to make it clear. "But I don't have a toothbrush or clothes for tomorrow ..."

"I've got plenty of toothbrushes. And I'll give you some clean socks and underwear."

"Then I'll stay."

He pulled my head to him with one hand and kissed me.

"Come on, let's go brush our teeth. It's time to hit the sack."

I followed him into the bathroom, smiling and excited. It had been a long time since an internet date had been so promising: good sex, then the invitation to spend the night (which meant he'd enjoyed it too), plus the offer to lend me a change of clothes (which presumed we'd see each other again so I could return them) .... In the bathroom, he opened one of the drawers under the sink. And I saw that he had dozens of extra toothbrushes, every one of them still in the package.

"Are you a dentist?" I asked, jokingly. "Or should I assume you score a lot?"

He didn't answer right away and, looking at his face in the mirror, I realized I might not want to hear his answer.

"I had a good time," he said, finally. "And if you want to stay over tonight, that's great. But don't go creating some fantasy situation here, OK?"

My mouth suddenly felt dry and at the same time all gummy after our lovemaking.

I wanted to run away, return home. But I also wanted to stay, hoping perhaps to recuperate what we had shared until I stuck my foot in it.

"Of course," I said, with a somewhat forced smile, and I held out the new toothbrush for him to give me a little bit of paste.

MY OWN CLASSIFICATION

On porn sites, whether they're free or for pay, the labels—twink, bare-back, three-ways, blow jobs, interracial, double penetration, etc.—never coincide with what turns me on. It all seems so cold to me, the actors (both the guy doing the fucking and the one being fucked) so serious in their determination, the moans so fake …. There's no human warmth. So I have to open all the links, take a look at all the galleries, fast forward through every video, searching for what excites me: guys who smile or laugh while they're fucking, unexpected flashes, any instant of humanity that sneaks into the filming …. Those are the moments that turn me on, the ones I add to my list of favorites so I can return to them when I'm home alone and feel the need to jerk off: me, my hand, and the screen lending some humanity.

LOST AND FOUND

The line snaked down a dark hallway and turned the corner. While I was walking to the back of it, I looked at the men standing single file, as if they were a mirror where I hoped to find a reflection of my own face. But I didn't recognize myself in them, nor did I feel complicity with any of them. That's why I'd come here.

The line crept along, and in the meantime, other men joined it behind me.

I passed the time thinking about other things, wondering every once in a while what I was going to find inside there. I recalled good times and imagined future possibilities and impossibilities. But the closer I got to the entrance, the more I was overcome by doubts and hopes, concerns and potentialities.

I studied the faces of the men who were exiting the doorway, but they disappeared before I could make out their faces, their moods.

It was finally my turn, and I crossed the doorway and entered the office with my heart pounding.

It was like any bureaucrat's office.

Behind the counter, a man, older than me, sitting in front of a computer.

Behind him, I saw one shelf after another, stacked high with cluttered objects piled on top of each other. Along the edges of the shelves, there were labels:

A Great Fuck
A Wild Stallion
The Love of My Life
Good Times
A Hungry Asshole
My Other Half
Hung Like a Horse

Chest Hair
A Knight in Shining Armor
Big Hands and Thick Wrists

The man behind the desk looked up from the computer screen and considered me slowly, before asking: "What're you looking for?"

HOT LINE

What are you wearing? That's how these conversations usually start, right? But I know what you're wearing: the blue suit your mom picked out. I didn't care. The whole funeral was a performance for her, so she could be the diva of grief because her son had been killed in a car accident. I was just a figurehead. My desire to have you cremated, your desire not to have a religious funeral, they didn't matter to her. It was easier to just give in, instead of fighting with her so I wouldn't miss you so much. Anyway. None of this is what I wanted to tell you when I called. Looks like I got sidetracked into complaining about your mother, just like I used to. Although it is thanks to her that I'm calling you; she was the one who suggested burying you with your cell phone, to be able to call you when she was missing you. And I'm finally calling. I know I'm talking to your voice mail, that you can't hear me, but ... I don't know, I wanted to talk to you, and it was easier to call you like this, I feel like less of an idiot than sitting home alone talking to you/to myself. I'm still so pissed at life, and at you, for abandoning me like that .... But I know I have to accept what happened, what's real. That's why I decided I need to fuck other men. Not to replace you, which isn't possible, but for me. To remember that I'm still alive and part of being alive is feeling desire, feeling desired. I haven't come since you died. I haven't even jerked off. Although I should confess that, hearing you again, your voicemail message, made me hard. I don't know, maybe I was predisposed, seeing as I was planning on talking with you about sex .... But it wasn't just that. I love you. I'll never forget you. But now I need to learn to live without you. I don't think it's going to be easy; just looking at another man still feels like a betrayal to me. But I'm going to try. I know it's what you would want for me. I still don't know who to do it with. Maybe we could try to pick someone ... together. As if it were a three-way, although only with your memory. If you want, we could fantasize about it together right now. I know you liked that neighbor across the way, we talked about it a few times. Maybe he should be the first one I let myself be seduced by, someone familiar …. Or would you want it to be someone anonymous, an impersonal fling, just what I need so I can stop thinking so much, analyzing so much, someone who can bend me over a table and …. *Beep beep.* I can't believe it; you're dead and our phone sex is interrupted by an incoming call. It's got to be your mother. She always did have a sixth sense for interrupting us when we were fucking, and the fact that you're dead hasn't changed that. I'll let you go, so she can talk to you. My hand and I will continue on our own. I love you.

BURSITIS

"That's it for today," the assistant told me, removing the ice from both my arms. "I'll see you tomorrow."

I massaged my right elbow while making my way to the changing room; my arm was half-asleep from the cold, but it still ached.

There was only one other patient in the changing room. I wasn't sure what he was being seen for, but when I arrived every day, he was sitting spread-eagled on top of a rubber triangle on one of the tables, some electrodes connected to the insides of his thighs. He was impeccably dressed, with a shirt that seemed too elegant for a physical therapy center, and even though he put shorts on for his treatment, he still wore loafers and socks up to his knees.

I dipped my head by way of greeting and turned toward the lockers. I was trying to open mine without hurting my elbow when I noticed a hand touching my crotch.

"What are you doing?" I asked.

"I heard you tell the physical therapist that since you hurt your right elbow you've developed tendinitis in your left hard from doing everything with that arm. So I'm going to give you a helping hand."

He'd pulled my zipper down while explaining all that. I was looking at him, and I still couldn't figure him out. He had a hipster moustache, but his look was pretty preppy. The truth is he wasn't really my type. I was going to keep on protesting, but he had my dick in his hand, and I was hard and ready to go, so I turned until my hips were facing him.

He gave me a smile and started stroking.

MY NEXT BEST SELLER

It was still too early to go to a bar like Hot, so we went into the VIPS at Plaza Callao to kill time. Glancing at the tables of books, Toni picked one up and said: "You should do something like this for your next book."

I looked at what he was holding in his hand: *The Year of Living Biblically*.

"I've heard of it. Some guy tries to follow the literal rules of the Bible for a year. All these books have some kind of gimmick, a concept or idea that hooks people. Like this one where the woman spends a year cooking every recipe in Julia Child." I showed him the book, *Julie & Julia*, with the new movie poster cover.

"Well then, you should think of some big concept so you can sell millions of copies."

"I can't imagine doing anything every day for a whole year. Except fucking, of course."

"Well there you go. You can spend a year trying to do all the positions in the *Kamasutra*."

"Ha! And if they don't want to publish it in the end?"

"What difference does that make? The research itself would be worth your while!"

BARISTA

I was ordering a coffee when I got distracted.

He was tall and imposing, and he knew it.

I wasn't the only one watching him make his way across the cafeteria to the door, we were all absorbing every detail: the biceps emphasized by the sleeve of his form-fitting t-shirt, his broad back and narrow waist forming a perfect triangle, his tight ass. An extraordinary specimen of masculinity.

When I looked back at the barista, he was watching me contemplate that super stud with a smile and waiting for me to finish ordering.

"Sorry," I said, blushing so hard I was sure my face was the color of a beet.

"No worries," the barista said. "He's a sight for sore eyes, that's for sure, but I bet he's super boring in the sack."

If possible, I blushed even harder.

"Why do you think?"

"I can figure out a lot about people by what they order and how they order. You just have to take a look at him to know that he spends his whole life rejecting pleasure: with his diet, the hours in the gym, the supplements and everything he takes to achieve and maintain that body. And he ordered a decaf cappuccino with skim milk and saccharine instead of sugar. Is that kind of artificial combination even worth ordering? In any case, it's a clear sign of wanting everything but being afraid to enjoy it."

On the one hand, I was paying attention to what he was telling me, but on the other, I was wondering what the drink I had begun to order said about me.

"But then, take a guy like that one over there as an example," he pointed at a bear sitting all alone at a table. "He ordered a café con leche, totally normal. But he also ordered a chocolate brownie, and when I asked him if he wanted it with whipped cream, he said: 'Why not?' That's the type of guy who's not afraid of enjoying the pleasures of life. I'm sure he'd be fun in bed. He'd give himself over completely to whatever he was doing."

I continued observing the guy. I wouldn't have looked at him before then, but now that I was paying attention, the truth is that he was kind of attractive. He was dressed in a plaid shirt, his beard was well groomed and enhanced the lines of his face, framing his smile. He wasn't fat, but he was heavy-set. What Yiddish grandmothers always call "zaftig," which I had never understood until now. He was *zaftig*.

When I turned back to the barista, he was watching how I was examining that nicely husky guy.

I started blushing again.

"Did you want anything else with your cortado?"

"I changed my mind," I said, trying to keep my voice under control, even though I couldn't suppress a smile. "Give me a café con leche. And a chocolate brownie, por favor."

Then I took the tray and, even though there were a lot of empty tables in the cafeteria, I approached the table where the bear was sitting and asked him: "Is this seat taken?"

HOMO LOGIC TEST

If Juan has thirteen beers and nine condoms, how many friends should he invite over tonight?

DEAR DIARY

Today while Álvaro was at work, I finally got the Polish guy who's remodeling the apartment on the first floor to fuck me ...

After writing the entry, I left my diary in its usual spot, where I knew Álvaro would find it and read it, and I went out to get groceries. I ran into the Polish guy in the downstairs hallway and greeted him with a "Buenos días." He responded politely in kind. We'd never fucked, even though I would have liked to, but it didn't matter: I knew my husband and I were going to have one hell of a ride that night, which is what always happens when he reads in my diary that I've been unfaithful .... He never says anything, not with words, but with sex ... with sex he does make it clear that he needs me and lays claim to me, dominating my whole body, leaving no doubt that I'm all his.

PORN SEQUENCE

I thought for years that I wasn't interested in porn. It's not that watching other people fuck didn't excite me. A friend complained that there was too much sex going on in the showers at his gym, and I signed up the next day, not to lose weight or build muscle, but to enjoy moments of being a voyeur (and at times participant) in sex scenes that were furtive and more exciting exactly because of the possibility that someone might walk in on them. Because voyeurs like me, those of us who're there when things start happening, we're an essential part of the scene.

I knew, therefore, that I liked and was excited by watching sex, but porn flicks left me cold ... until I discovered the French director Cadinot. I happened upon one of his movies by accident, having a drink in some seedy dive that projected videos on a small screen above the bar. They were normally like visual white noise for me, and in this case, I was pretty uninterested right off the bat because the actors were very young and very clean-shaven, no matter how big their dicks were.

But since there wasn't anyone in the bar who interested me, and partly because I wanted to seem unavailable to this one jerk who kept looking at me, I started watching the movie.

And I realized all of a sudden that it was a single long take. And to my surprise, I started getting excited as I watched it.

What Cadinot was doing, besides telling stories where the sex often advanced the plot rather than interrupting the narrative, was film real sex. His camera let us be voyeurs, au naturel, without all the jump cuts that porn tends to use, especially at the moment of penetration. Close-up of a cock pushing against the other guy's asshole and one second later, full-on fucking with a condom on. They make me feel manipulated, and they break the spell for me, like when you're reading a book and all of a sudden there's an anachronism or a mistake, something that doesn't fit, which makes you remember you're reading a book instead of living the adventure that it contains.

Cadinot seduced me so successfully that I didn't realize that the jerk from the bar had come over until I felt his hand on my crotch. I looked around, but no one more interesting had shown up yet. I didn't encourage him, but I didn't do anything to stop him either as he unzipped my pants, took out my cock and kneeled down in front of me to suck me off.

I watched Cardinot's long take while offering up a scene for the voyeurs in the bar.

THE MORNING AFTER

"Well, well, well," said the waitress.

"What?"

"You're smiling from ear to ear. I think someone got lucky last night."

I blushed. When you stop in at the same place every morning on the way to work, they get to know you pretty well after a while … and not only that you take your coffee with two sugars.

"It's true," I confessed. "And to celebrate, why don't you give me a chocolate donut as well."

"I'm happy for you," she said, handing me my pastry before turning to another customer who came in after me.

In the mirror behind the counter, I saw that I was still grinning from ear to ear. And it was because, even though she hadn't asked for details from last night (we were friendly, but not that much), I couldn't stop thinking about it: kissing in the disco, his eagerness to get my clothes off when I invited him home, the brush of his skin against my skin between the sheets, the care with which he placed the condom on me and then the sweet pleasure of sinking into him …

After we came, I went into the kitchen to grab a couple of beers, which we shared in bed before he left.

A lovely night, like I hadn't experienced in a long time, that had left me with such a good taste in my mouth that even the waitress recognized it the next morning.

I finished my coffee, ready to dive into my day and head to the office.

I took out my wallet to pay and was left completely flabbergasted.

"What's wrong?" she asked in a worried tone of voice. "You look like you saw a ghost."

I looked up slowly and showed her my wallet.

"My fling from last night ripped me off!"

"That bastard! Don't worry about this, my treat," the waitress insisted.

That was the good thing about going to the same place every morning.

I walked toward the office like a zombie, unable to believe what had happened. Or when it had happened. It had to have been when I went to get the beer. That was the only time I left him alone. And it had been so brief ... I could almost remember the exact moment: me, in the kitchen, with the door to the fridge open, imagining him lying on the bed relaxing in a post-coital haze, while he, in reality, was secretly digging through the pockets of the pants that he'd pulled off me just minutes earlier.

THE TOWER OF BABEL

They say the best way to learn a language is in bed ... but I hate feeling like I need to find a language school so I can hook up in my own country. When did gay guys all suddenly decide to speak English ... at least on their profiles. I don't know if they're on a search and capture mission for tourists, having already plundered everything the local market has to offer, or if they just want to flaunt their worldliness ... but it strikes me as pretty pathetic. And of course, they're still total hicks when they snd a txt about their PEN15 even after changing the language. God!

What a pleasure to click on a profile and see that it's all in Spanish, be able to start a conversation and not have to find a dictionary to specify what we feel like doing, when and where.

The worst part are the acronyms. I don't understand them half the time in Spanish, so it's awful to try to figure out the profile of some German or French dude who's visiting Madrid, whether TBM Ffun mec NSA PNP or any other code in that alphabet soup of sexuality is what he is or what he's looking for.

I don't have anything against foreigners.

Quite the contrary, I find a lot of them very attractive, and they can take me to places sexually that I wouldn't explore any other way.

And in person, it doesn't matter if we don't speak the same language.

Because the only language I want to talk is body language, my tongue touching yours, your body whispering all its secrets to me.

AROUND THE CAMPFIRE

The night had cooled off when the sun went down, but what made my hair stand on end was the stories we told around the campfire, each one more terrifying than the last, or that's how it seemed to me. Everyone else was laughing, making jokes, but I've always had an over-active imagination and I couldn't help but experience every story as if I were the one starring in it until the frightful end.

Later, alone in my tent, I couldn't get to sleep: every crackle of the logs on the fire, every insect that struck the plastic, every sound reminded me of those ghost stories and I imagined a thousand monsters that were coming to kill me.

When I heard footsteps quietly approaching my tent, I thought my heart would stop. *They're just stories*, I told myself, squeezing my eyes closed, *they're not true*. But then I heard something scraping against the tent. *If I don't pay attention, it'll go away*, I thought. A voice whispered my name, and I almost fainted. Until I realized it was Peter's voice, and he was outside.

"Very funny," I told him when he unzipped the tent and slipped in alongside me. "You almost gave me a heart attack."

"Sorry," he apologized. "It wasn't a joke. I'm scared and I don't want to sleep alone. Can I stay with you?"

I opened the sleeping bag to share it with him. He lay down by my side, and we tried to get comfortable in the tight space. His legs were freezing, I wasn't sure if it was from fear or from cold, but they warmed up quickly. I wasn't listening to the sounds outside the tent any more, I was only focused on his breathing, his head so close to mine.

Just when I was wondering if he had fallen asleep, he whispered: "I'm not scared anymore."

"Me either," I said.

His hand reached for mine inside the sleeping bag. And then in silence, we shared a tale of the living instead of stories about the undead.

FAIRY TALE

"What big eyes you have!"

 "The better to see you get naked," I said.

 "What big ears you have!"

 "The better to hear you moan when you come," I said.

 "And what a big mouth you have!"

 "The better to eat you all up."

 And, like the wolf, that's what I did, devouring his reddish glans covered by its foreskin-hood.

NOSTALGIA

There are streets I rarely walk down, and one of them is Lavapiés itself, even though I've been living in that neighborhood for a few years now. I live almost on the edge of where Distrito Centro turns into Arganzuela on the Ronda de Valencia. Years ago, it didn't bother me to go up or down any street, no matter how steep, but it's harder for me now and I tend to take the metro or the bus. But it's a beautiful afternoon, so after taking care of a few errands around Plaza del Sol, I decided to walk back home and I found myself wandering down Lavapiés and remembering, a decade earlier, when I would be on that same street all the time because I had a boyfriend who lived on Ministriles, a small parallel street. We were constantly coming and going between our two apartments to spend the night together or just to get laid. It was his first apartment as a single guy, so I gave him my IKEA futon (I still got to use it on the nights we spent together anyway), and I bought myself a new bed. He was shorter than me and I remembered how our bodies fit together perfectly, as if they were melting into each other.

Since I was thinking about him, my first reaction was that the guy on the corner where I always used to turn to get to Ministriles only looked like him because my memory was playing tricks on me. But as I got closer, the impression didn't weaken, and I suddenly found myself in front of him. He greeted me like a ghost rising up out of my nostalgia, but a decade older, with gray hair sprinkled throughout his beard and on his head, not like it was back then. The connection between us was as strong as ever and when he hugged and kissed me, there in the middle of the street, it was as if I had entered my own past.

Except for one thing. We no longer fit together like we used to.

He smiled at me when we stopped kissing, and his hands slid down to rest on my spare tire.

"What are you doing here? Last I saw, on Facebook, you were still in Zaragoza ..."

"I'm in town for a meeting. My train's in a few hours, but since I had some free time, I was taking a walk around the old neighborhood."

"My current neighborhood," I told him, "I live right at the bottom of the hill."

While we were walking, we talked about our lives, our jobs, our current partners.

We went up to my place and, before you know it, we had our clothes off and were in the bedroom. I wasn't young enough to fuck on futons or sofas anymore.

I grabbed a condom from the nightstand, and he put it on.

He entered me, and it was just like I remembered. In fact, while the pleasure expanded throughout my body, I didn't know where the current pleasure ended and all those moments of remembered pleasure began.

Because, in spite of my belly, some things still fit together perfectly.

FAMILY DINNER

"I think you've made a conquest," said my mother-in-law.

"What are you talking about?" I replied.

"That boy in the corner hasn't taken his eyes off you since we sat down. If he could, he'd be over here eating with you, and you'd be the main course."

It's not that my mother-in-law is vulgar, but she can be very direct. We still hadn't gotten together very often, although we'd been making an effort to see each other more frequently since Brad and I got married a few months earlier.

"I can't turn around to look and see if I know him."

"I think he knows you, but not vice versa," said Brad.

"Or at least, he recognizes you and wants to meet you," affirmed my mother-in-law.

It might seem strange that someone who's acted in porn flicks would be embarrassed by a situation like this. But while Brad knew about that part of my past (we'd even watched a few of my films together), it was different to talk about these things in front of his mother, even though she already knew about my films too (I thought it was better to confess it to her than to have some rumormongers drag her son-in-law through the mud in the future). She didn't make a big deal out of it, but we didn't all sit down to watch them as a family either!

"Why don't you go to the bathroom? I bet he follows you," suggested my mother-in-law.

"And if he follows me?"

It always bothers me when people think that because I've done porn, I'd fuck anybody.

"That's up to you," she replied, calmly. "I'm sure you'd brighten up his evening. And he's pretty good-looking, right, son?"

"He's hot," Brad declared, smiling when he saw how uncomfortable the situation had made me.

It would have been easier to turn around, even if it was blatant. But by now I was intrigued and, among other things, I wanted to see if the guy would follow me like my mother-in-law had predicted. I don't know if I wanted to prove something to her or to myself.

"Do you mind?" I asked Brad, setting my napkin on the table and getting ready to stand up.

"Of course not," he replied. "We can entertain ourselves until you get back."

"And when you get back, you can tell us everything," said my mother-in-law.

I got up and, without looking around, I walked toward the bathroom.

HYPOCHONDRIAC

"Look at this. What do you think it is?"

"Nothing."

"Are you sure?"

"So sure that I'm going to put it in my mouth, see?"

While I sucked his dick, I realized that he showed up with a different "medical" pretext to drop his pants every day, and I began to wonder if, instead of a hypochondriac, he was a nymphomaniac …

PROVOCATION

During the first beer, he complained about his girlfriend.

During the second, he got nostalgic and began to miss her.

Halfway through the third, he looked me in the eye and asked: "Is a blow job by a dude different than a blow job by a girl?"

I took a long swig without breaking eye contact, before reaching out my hand and starting to unbutton his fly. "There's only one way to find out."

BALCONY FISHING

When I went to see the apartment, my friend Esteban advised me not to rent it, warning me that anything on the second floor of Calle Hortaleza would be very loud. I have earplugs, so I didn't care, but I used that excuse to convince the landlord to reduce the rent around 40 euros. I bet he's gotten a lot of complaints or renters who break the contract because the noise is driving them crazy, because he agreed without hesitating. I probably could have bargained him down even further.

But for me, it's an ideal location. Every night, around three in the morning, I go out onto the balcony. All the guys who didn't manage to hook up over in Cruising spill out onto the streets, their balls still full and their standards nearly scraping the ground. And from up on high, I get to take my pick, judging not only by their appearance but also the way they move, their level of sex-appeal. When one of them interests me, I whistle, and they look up and see the light.

And when they leave, after we've had sex, I put my earplugs in and sleep like a log.

WHERE WE GOING?

I've been on the corner for more than ten minutes, but every taxi that goes by is already taken.

The light turns red, and another taxi with a passenger stops right in front of me.

"Where you going?" the driver asks me through his window.

I tell him.

"OK, get in," he motions, and I don't hesitate. I sit in front, putting on the seatbelt.

The other passenger, an American, is going to Chamartín Station. He says he met a Spanish girl in a bar tonight, and she kissed him on the mouth. He asks if all Spanish girls are that forward.

I notice how the bulge in the driver's pants is growing. He sees me observing him.

We drop the foreigner off at the station.

"Where we going?" he asks.

I reach out my hand and place it on his thigh.

He smiles at me and turns off the meter.

CONNECTION

I had time to kill in Hamburg, and at that time of night, everything was closed except for a McDonalds and a Beate Uhse, that chain of German sex shops. I wasn't horny when I walked in the door, just bored. I'd gotten something to eat at the McDonalds, even though I wasn't hungry, so I could sit and wait for a while, but my train still wasn't leaving for two hours.

As I walked inside, I nodded at the guy behind the counter, but I didn't pay much attention to him. Looking someone in the eye is an invitation, especially in a place like this.

I wasn't looking to buy anything either, nor did I have the money to do so. I was traveling through Europe for a month on an InterRail pass, sleeping on night trains so I wouldn't have to pay for hotels. But some routes required a supplement for the direct train, which is why I found myself here, at this time of night, killing time.

I went up and down the aisles, looking at what they were selling. Everything was for sale here, and nothing was hidden. I thought about what they say happens to people who work in chocolate factories: for the first few weeks, you're drooling all the time, but after a while, you get immune to it. I looked at the guy behind the counter, wondering whether the same thing had happened to him, if his cock was hard for 8 hours at a time for the first month, but after seeing so many hard dicks and tits and asses on the covers of videos and on screens, the dildos and handcuffs and everything else, nothing could shock or excite him anymore.

To my surprise, the guy was looking at me, and I saw his arm moving slowly beneath the counter. Was he jacking off? I was the only customer. I doubted that he liked me so much that he couldn't help jerking off. Instead, I imagined he was just tired of being alone.

The truth of the matter is that I wasn't that attracted to him; I prefer guys who are shorter than me, indie guys, with tattoos and piercings. He was on the big side, like a bouncer at a disco, with a shaved head and an earring in one ear. If I'd ever fantasized about being with a gladiator …

But I had time to kill. I approached the counter. He lifted his dick with one hand so I could see it better. It was big, like him, and ramrod straight, with a head that was nearly square beneath the foreskin. Mine was thinner, and curved, with a glans that perched like a beret on top of a pole. I looked up and nodded yes.

He didn't say anything but got up from his stool and approached the door. He locked it, and for a moment, a shiver ran through my body, between fear and excitement. He replaced the sign on the door with one that said ZURÜCK IN 5 MINUTEN. I followed him to a booth, hoping we would take longer than that. I needed to kill time without falling asleep and missing my train.

LUCK OF THE DRAW

I was happy with life that spring. I liked my job and had two regular lovers, so I was sexually satisfied without having to spend nights of frustrated searching.

I had met Fran at La Casa de la Portera. We'd both gone with friends, but the play didn't interest us that much. We spent the first act looking at each other instead of the actors, and we started talking during intermission. We changed seats for the second act, and if it weren't for the fact that the theater was such a small space, we would have started getting friendly right then and there. Our friends insisted on getting something to drink with their actor friends after the play. I went down to the bathroom, and he came down shortly thereafter. He was a good kisser so I invited him home, and he fucked equally well. Since he wasn't insistent or clingy, I invited him to spend the night. That's how we started staying together some nights, enjoying ourselves, but without overwhelming each other by formalizing what we had with labels or exclusivity.

Alberto didn't pressure me to have a relationship beyond sex either because he already had a partner. We met online one night, and I went to his place. His partner, who worked as an aide in a hospital, had a rotating shift: he worked four afternoons, then two nights, followed by two days off, so his schedule changed every week. What was most important to me were the nights he worked, which I sometimes took advantage of to visit Alberto. Not always, since that would have been too much responsibility. But I admit that I liked it that he was available on a regular, predictable schedule. In fact, on more than one occasion, feeling in the mood but also lazy, I texted him to arrange a visit for the following night, rather than going out looking.

They weren't the only men I had sex with, but they were the regulars. And the two of them were different enough that I didn't get bored.

Months went by. Fran found a new apartment, and I didn't see him for some time, while he was moving and then getting settled in. I got a promotion at work. I went out with some friends to celebrate, but a lot of them had partners and family and could only stay for a few beers. I was walking back to the metro to go home when I got a text: *i'm moved in, when do you want to give the new bed a try? fran.*

I called him and we agreed to meet fifteen minutes later by the Lavapiés metro. We got a bite to eat, and then he took me to his apartment. It was a route I knew well. That would be funny, I thought. Until he was opening *that* door to the street and it didn't seem so humorous anymore. I was hoping to avoid a meeting that would be ... uncomfortable, even though I didn't have anything to hide or apologize for. We got into the elevator and my stomach sank when he pushed the button for the fourth floor. What were the chances? I knew that things had been going too well for me.

And that was the truth. Just as Fran was opening door D, door C opened.

"Hola, Alberto," I said.

VICE VERSA

I don't have a lot of patience for profiles that are full of song lyrics and poetry. And it's not because I don't like poetry, quite the contrary, I'm a poet and that's why I treat it with a lot of respect. When I want to read poetry, I pick up a book. When I'm online, I want to hook up.

That's why I was going to close the profile without looking at it when a line caught my attention. Reading it again, I realized it was something I had written. And in fact, scrolling down through the text box on the profile, it cited my name.

What a curious experience. I didn't know whether to greet him and reveal that I was the author of his poem or not.

But the worst of it was: I no longer felt like having sex.

Finding those verses of mine made me transition from being the ordinary guy that I am, with sexual desires like any other guy, to the public persona of a writer ... whose photo appears on the cover of the book where that poem came from. If he looked at his track list to see who had visited his profile, he was sure to recognize me. But if he tried to meet up with me, it would be with the writer, with his experience of having read me, with everything that he projected onto me from that reading. Not with the guy who until a few minutes ago was horny and looking for a pleasurable roll in the hay with no strings attached ...

I decided to turn off the computer and jerk off. And then, since I wasn't going to go out tonight, I'd read some poems.

SHARED CODES

There aren't many of us who go to record stores, and out of that minority, there are even fewer of us who like to fuck other guys. That's why I almost didn't pay attention to him as he sifted through the international CDs in the basement of Metralleta. I thought "what a cutie" and continued running my fingers along the spines of the albums while I read the names of titles and groups.

But out of the corner of my eye, I realized he was in the national CD section. And that made me curious. Nowadays, a young guy like him would normally be looking at LPs, a format that had risen from the ashes like a Phoenix because of the hipsters. He looked so young that he must have been one of those digital natives who don't even know what CDs are for, having grown up in the age of MP3 players and Spotify. There aren't too many of us who still listen to (or buy) CDs. And that's obvious by how little merchandise reaches second-hand stores like Metralleta anymore.

Even though, in theory and in practice, we can pick people up anywhere, whether in the streets or in a supermarket, I felt a little bit out of place thinking about him sexually in there. It was the collision of two worlds that had been separated for me until now. If we had met up in the bathrooms on the top floor of the FNAC, just a few meters from here, it would have seemed like the most natural thing in the world. Even if we'd been at the Rastro flea market, searching through adjacent boxes of records, it would have been a more open environment, or at least, one where the possibility of hooking up was more expected, more habitual. But now I felt exposed, as if the girl at the cash register and the other guys had caught us *in flagrante delicto* ... But I had only looked at him, I'd only wondered to myself if he was gay.

Suddenly he raised his eyes and looked at me directly, as if he could feel my gaze and my interest. I forced a smile and started rummaging through the CDs again, embarrassed that he had caught me. But I was no longer seeing the titles or the groups, and I started undressing him with my imagination.

My hands began to sweat. I wasn't sure if I was interested because I liked him physically (I tend to prefer guys who are older than him, no matter how cute he was) or because of the novelty of finding an attractive guy who liked music. Should I try to talk to him? I already had the "no," but what if he said "yes"? … He could be a dream come true. I took a deep breath to work up my courage and crossed the aisle to the section of national CDs, where he was now, almost at the end of the alphabet.

"Do you know this one?" said someone by my side. I was so startled my heart almost stopped beating: it was him. He'd taken the first step. His voice was deeper than I expected. Maybe he wasn't as young as I thought.

He had *Planes de verano* by Algora in his hand. A clear signal for me.

"A real gem," I answered, and I returned his smile.

OVERHEARD

He hurried out of the stall, his eyes averted, and only stopped when he got to the door that led to the dance floor. Some guy almost ran into Alberto, who was coming out of the same stall, in no hurry whatsoever, buckling the belt under his prominent belly while he crossed the bathroom over to where Ernesto was waiting for him.

"Sorry," whispered Ernesto, "I always seem to shout when I come. Do you think any of them heard us?"

Alberto turned his head slowly to look at the line of guys waiting to pee, almost the entire line looking back at them, and finally answered: "Hopefully all of them!"

DEATH IN IBIZA

How much loyalty do we owe someone simply because we've had sex with them?

This was the question I kept returning to, between customer and customer, while I asked myself what to do with the guy who was in the storeroom.

We'd met two nights earlier, in Angelo's, where I had stopped for a beer before heading home. I wasn't planning on hooking up with anyone, but sometimes it's hard not to during high season, especially there, at the foot of the path that goes up to D'Alt Villa. I couldn't remember the name of Graeme's friend, even though he was the one who started talking to me. They were interchangeable: just two more British tourists, barely twenty years old, during a 3-day weekend abroad. I scored with one of them. And now the other one was dead. Even though one thing had nothing to do with the other, except that Graeme, the guy I'd fucked, reappeared in my life when he showed up at the store this morning begging for help.

He told me the story in bits and pieces. Every time a customer came in, Graeme acted all nervous. In any other location, that type of behavior would have awoken suspicions, but in my store, it was a typical reaction for a certain type of customer who's embarrassed to be seen buying a dildo or lube.

From what I understood, Graeme took some guy back to the apartment he'd rented with that friend whose name I couldn't remember. The door to the other room was closed when they got there from the bar, so Graeme thought his friend had picked someone up as well. In the morning, since the door was still closed, he knocked, and since there wasn't any answer, he opened it, to find his friend alone in the bed with a knife in his back.

His boy toy from the previous evening got hysterical: "I can't believe it! We spent the night sleeping right next door to a cadaver!" He took off running, saying he was going to call the police.

Graeme got out of there as fast as he could as well. He didn't know what had happened to his friend, but since he didn't speak a word of Spanish, he was afraid of the cops, especially since he and his friend had bought some drugs when they arrived.

So he fled the scene of the crime and came directly to my door.

I'm not sure why I let him stay.

He meant nothing to me. I wasn't in any hurry to repeat the sex we'd had, and neither was he, given that he'd picked up that other guy ...

But at two o'clock, when I closed the store for lunch, I went into the storeroom. Graeme looked at me with a mixture of hope and fear, like a dog that's been beaten.

I unbuttoned the fly of my jeans and took out my dick.

Graeme kneeled down in front of me without saying a word.

I still wasn't sure if I owed him anything or not, but since he'd gotten me mixed me up in this whole mess, I could at least make it worth my while ...

MACHINE WASH

"I can't find any clean glasses," said Eric while he rummaged through the kitchen cabinets.

"Look in the dishwasher," shouted Ángel from the other room.

A few minutes later, Ángel appeared in the kitchen, asking: "Did you find them?" as he discovered Eric, dumbfounded, in front of the open dishwasher. On the top tray, in addition to the clean glasses, there were four dildos of different sizes and colors. Eric was holding the fifth in his hand.

"And these?" asked Eric.

"Haven't you ever used one?" answered Ángel.

"Certainly not!" he replied immediately.

"The only thing that's certain is that you'd like to give it a try," Ángel said, stretching his hand out over the open door of the dishwasher that separated them, to touch the evidence of Eric's state of excitement.

"Come on, bring the rest of them," continued Ángel, picking two out of the tray, "and I'll show you how to use them."

He moved toward the bedroom, and a moment later, Eric appeared with the other dildos. Ángel organized them on top of the bedspread, from smallest to largest.

"Have you used all of them?" Eric asked, staring at the display in front of them.

"They're clean," answered Ángel, starting to unbutton his shirt. "Pick one. You can even use them all. That's what the dishwasher's for!"

LA PETITE MORT

He collapsed like a dead man after coming, and if it weren't for his snoring, I might have worried that he had suffered something more serious than an orgasm. The Romans used to place coins on the eyes of the dead so they could pay Charon to ferry them to Hades. I reached out my hand and grabbed two condoms from the nightstand, in their silvery square packages. I placed them on top of his closed eyelids, wishing him erotic dreams after the little death we had shared.

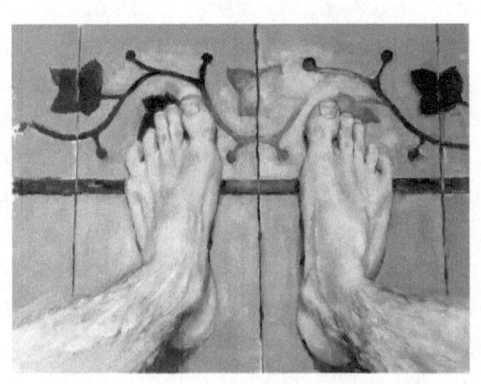

SECOND COFFEE

When I got home, Antonio had already had his first coffee of the morning, but he still hadn't taken a shower.

"Morning, Sweetie," I said as I entered the kitchen, where he was standing, wearing a robe that covered his shoulders but was untied, grinding the beans to prepare a second pot. I'd be happy with instant, but Antonio was a perfectionist when it came to coffee. Or actually, in every aspect of his (and our) life.

"You have fun?" he asked, but it was more of a greeting than a question, because before I could answer, he threw himself at me: his tongue, that tasted like Arabica beans, was exploring my mouth and preventing my answer, and while I melted in his arms, his large hands, warmed by the mug, slid under the waistband on my sweat pants to fondle my ass. With his first and second fingers together, he found my asshole, and I moaned when his fingers gently slipped inside me; I'd washed up before leaving Odarko, but I was still lubricated. His erection grew, squeezed hot between our bodies, reclaiming me after not sleeping together that night. A third finger joined the other two. He broke off our kiss to spit on his other hand and lubricate his hard dick with his saliva. Neither the furniture nor my back would withstand me lying on the countertop with my feet in the air (a cliché straight out of so many porn flicks), and the urgency of his desire didn't allow for those kinds of acrobatics.

He turned my whole body, and at the same time as he was pushing my torso, he plunged all the way inside me, with a grunt of pleasure and effort.

Antonio is truly a perfectionist, but he could also be a total brute when the moment, like now, required it. And I gave myself over to him completely, my whole being was a vehicle to pleasure him.

He came with a shout and collapsed on top of me, his breath tickling my ear while he tried to catch his breath. His chest was pinning my body

100

against the marble, and the folds of his robe hung down on each side as if they could cover both of us.

I couldn't count the number of guys who had fucked me that night in the sex club, but those were nothing more than preliminary games for this morning shag with my husband.

With his hot semen inside me, I prepared Antonio's second pot of coffee while he showered and got dressed for the office.

MARKED TERRITORY

Gorka finished his coffee and stood up.

"I've got some things to do," he said, before giving his husband a kiss on the lips and waving goodbye to me from his side of the table. Then he added: "Nice to meet you, Luis. Enjoy yourselves."

When he had gone, I turned to Aitor and asked him: "It really doesn't bother him?"

"Why would it bother him?"

"Well … Since he wanted to meet me and all …"

Aitor laughed.

"Before you and I fuck, you mean. That was more for you than for anything. So you don't get the wrong idea about what's going on between us. He's my husband and we really love each other, which doesn't prevent us from enjoying other men too."

"And when he has a pickup, do you go meet them too?"

"Of course. Neither of us gets jealous. And we don't want to stop being together. But we also like to have some experiences outside of our relationship. Why would we want to stop our partner from having more pleasure in his life?"

I felt odd, maybe because the situation was new to me. Intellectually I understood it, but emotionally was another thing. I felt baffled. Aitor, sitting next to me in the coffee shop, was really attractive—he was sexier in person than in the photos on his profile—and I didn't understand why it didn't bother Gorka that, according to what we'd all agreed on, in less than an hour Aitor and I would be fucking. I felt conflicted. I felt desire on the one hand, but confusion on the other.

And also maybe disappointment. Because, even though I knew that Aitor had a partner from the beginning, I'd only thought about it in the abstract. But now that I'd met him, I couldn't ignore the reality anymore.

"Hey, why the long face?" said Aitor, signaling the waiter to bring the check. "We're going to have a good time, you'll see."

We paid the bill and I followed him to his apartment, which was very close to the coffee shop where we'd met. Climbing the stairs behind him, my attention swung between looking at the muscles in his ass underneath his shorts, an ass which I'd be able to disrobe and appreciate very soon, and thinking that they must do all of this so often that it was a routine now: meeting up in that coffee shop, which was close to home for them, and agreeing that their partner would make himself scarce for a while. I couldn't help looking around, seeking out evidence of their life together, while Aitor gave me the tour of their apartment, talking in first-person plural the whole time. And I realized that maybe their plan of action made sense, meeting up with the third ahead of time, making it all clear, like dogs marking their territory, even if they did invite guests into the mix.

I stopped obsessing about things I had never wanted until they were outside of my grasp. I approached Aitor, entering his personal space but without the slightest contact yet. He smiled at me, and I reached out to touch him. This was what I wanted; it's what I'd come for.

LOCATION

Over time, Salva had begun to hate GPS.

Checking out profiles on his cell phone, he only saw the same faces. At least, in the ones that included a face pic—at least as many of them only had anonymous dick pics, erect or not, or naked asses. It struck Salva as so ridiculous and the complete opposite of exciting. It stripped away part of the mystery of getting to know a guy, the romanticism of flirting, the approach and the mutual revelation until that moment when the two bodies would meld into one. If you even arrived at that point; not all dates had to culminate in sex. All of it was part of a way of discovering and exploring the world and the other men who inhabit it.

But that world was lost now, even though he continued living in it, strolling down its streets and searching for ... not simply men, or that special man, but perhaps that longed-for past in which proximity did not take precedence over all other considerations.

Global positioning had made Salva lose his way.

He felt constrained, restricted, limited.

There was a time in which he explored the entire city because of the dates he confirmed after sessions in chat rooms. He often remembered the early days of the internet when people, who still didn't have computers at home, would go to cybercafés to meet up and communicate. One of the biggest ones, in those days, was the EasyEverything on Montera Street, right by Madrid's Kilometer Zero, so large that it filled two stories and so cheap and centrally located that it was sometimes busier than some of the gay bars. There were times when some guy would stand up for a second and then sit back down, and everyone (or at least all the gay guys) knew he was flirting with someone who was there too .... Even though they all converged there, they would then go back (alone or with their new companions) to homes that were spread out around the city.

But now everyone had a cell phone or computer with GPS, and people were no longer seeking out soul mates, but the person who was closest at hand.

The worst of it was that, without those devices, people didn't exist. They didn't go to bars anymore, where they could be surprised by the unexpected, by someone they hadn't even imagined outside of their dreams .... Nobody bothered leaving home anymore when they could just get home delivery.

Salva was now becoming a *flâneur*, someone who wandered the city, randomly visiting neighborhoods in a type of cruising, not for sex, but for encounters that began with a meeting in some café.

His friends never knew where he was, and he tended to get WhatsApp messages, like now, messages asking:

WHERE YOU AT?

Salva responded, hitting "Share my location."

WITH A FRIEND YOU NEED TO MEET.

GPS wasn't always bad.

SOMMELIER

"Welcome to the dark room. I'm your sommelier this evening. Here are today's specials."

His flashlight illuminated a hole in the wall. A dick appeared, engorged but not completely hard. The foreskin was still completely covering the glans.

"This varietal has a slightly fruity bouquet, with a high concentrate of spermatozoids."

The next cock was fat with thick veins covering the shaft.

"You can see the body in this sample, or at least the part that's revealed here. A mature specimen, with a more complete flavor."

The light turned toward the next dick, which was long and thin, completely hard and straining to go.

"This tempranillo belongs to a young stallion, a bit sweet on the palate."

The flashlight continued revealing options until the sommelier realized they weren't paying attention to him anymore.

"I see you've made your first selections. But if you need any further recommendations ... or suggestions for good flavor combinations, I'm at your service."

BREATHLESS

Their relationship was so fleeting that the pick up and break up occurred in the same kiss.

He offered him a mint, asking: "Want one?" as the politest way to say: "You've got terrible breath."

Then he excused himself to go to the bathroom and took advantage of the opportunity to leave the bar where they had met and take deep breaths of the fresh night air.

PUPPY LOVE

It's not that I'm afraid of dogs, but they had never appealed to me before. When I saw this guy coming down the sidewalk toward me with a boxer, I suddenly wanted to be a canine specialist so I could strike up a conversation with him. I needn't have worried, because the dog was the one who broke the ice for us, bounding over to me and sticking his snout between my legs to sniff my balls—just what I wanted to do to his owner. I bent down to pet him, letting him lick my face, and in passing, I placed myself at eye-level with the guy's crotch. I very nearly stuck my nose between his legs, like his dog had done to me. But I controlled myself and asked him the dog's name and, thanks to Izko, we started talking so naturally that I almost didn't realize I'd managed to pick him up until we were going up to his apartment. We had to close the door to the bedroom so that Izko wouldn't interrupt us, and it didn't take long before I was able to stick my nose between his owner's legs, just like I wanted, making him wag his tail and perform other tricks as well.

I don't remember his name, I don't even know if I asked; I always remember him as Izko's owner. From that point on, it was clear to me that a dog could have a positive impact on my sex life …. The only thing was that I preferred visiting the flats of guys who had dogs instead of getting my own pet. And it almost always worked like that: since they had to let their dogs out and feed them, it was better to go with them to their place instead of inviting them to mine. That way, I could leave whenever I wanted, once we were done screwing and had enjoyed whatever post-intimacy we desired. When I started noticing dogs before their owners on my walks around Bilbao, I began to get worried; I was developing a fetish, or that's what it seemed like. Of course, I didn't hook up with all the guys with dogs that I met on the streets, although I wouldn't have minded if that had happened. The truth of the matter was that the guys who had dogs were more relaxed, in general, and their pets worked as the ideal pretext to stop them and start up a conversation. I no longer went to bars or looked for sex online, I walked around the city, almost as if I had my own dog, and that's how enjoyable encounters arose from time to time, sometimes with new guys and other times with guys whose dogs already recognized my scent.

One afternoon, I was leaning against the railing in front of the Jeff Koons sculpture outside the Guggenheim Museum. A couple of foreigners, tall and blond, approached me and asked in English about Puppy. When I later accompanied them to their hotel, I laughed: maybe I'd finally found my own dog.

VISITING HOME

Sergio tried not to look out the window of the train, but it made no difference: his anxiety grew the further south he went, even without seeing those key locations of the journey, those signposts that meant that he was returning to his hometown and his past. He felt as if every kilometer was erasing another aspect of the personal growth and development he had achieved since moving to the capital. The distance wasn't only physical, but also temporal, because people back home saw him not as he was (a gay man, single but at peace with his sexuality and his identity, with a job he liked and a group of friends with whom he really clicked) but the way he had been (the weird kid, neither accepted nor understood).

His brother Diego was waiting for him at the station. On the drive home, they made small talk—the trip, work, nieces and nephews—topics and details he would have to repeat thousands of times that weekend. No one would ask him if he was happy, if he had a boyfriend, the things that really mattered.

Crossing the main plaza, Sergio saw a young man, very attractive, carrying some plastic bags emblazoned with the logo of the fruit store. He didn't remember ever seeing him before. He wouldn't have minded being able to see him better and longer, instead of putting up with his family during an entire 3-day weekend. He didn't know how to ask his brother who the young man was without the question giving rise to too many other questions, so he remained silent until they got home.

"I invited some new neighbors over for dinner," his mother said, after she greeted him with a kiss. And Sergio began to feel a knot in his stomach: not only would he be unable to relax with his family, whose prejudices were at least known to him, but he would have to be friendly with strangers and put up with their interrogations.

He went up to his room, feeling like a tourist in his own past. He'd already rescued everything he wanted from there, and what remained was just dead weight that his mother took painstaking care of. He could now recognize that taking care of his things was her way of trying to show interest and concern for him; his family had never talked about their feelings easily.

The doorbell rang. Sergio gave a deep sigh and went down to face the firing squad.

"This is Manolo and Jimena," said his mother, introducing the new neighbors. "And this is their son Bruno."

It was the guy he had seen in the plaza with the bags from the fruit store!

Once he'd gotten over the surprise of meeting him—something he had desired but ruled out as impossible—Sergio realized he wasn't only attractive, but also single and gay. Because their two sets of parents had organized this whole thing, a pretext to introduce their sons to see if they would hit it off.

They still didn't talk about certain subjects, but maybe his hometown really was changing, like his mother was always telling him. And maybe his family was as well.

CONTROL

For a lot of guys, sex equals ejaculation, but I don't even touch myself when I'm with someone. What's most important to me is the feeling of control. There are a lot of people who think that being a cocksucker means being passive, but that idea could not be further from the truth. It is true that there are guys who like to fuck my mouth, holding my jaw to immobilize my face while their cocks penetrate my lips like pistons .... But even with them, I'm the ultimate reason that they come. I'm the one who worships their manhood, adoring them with my tongue, devouring them to the very end, no matter how big or small they are .... I'm the one who idolizes them, and they are always the object of admiration.

The fact that my mouth is capable of provoking their salty burst of pleasure, whether they're rich snobs or construction workers, old dudes or teenagers, if they've got hairy beer bellies or are smooth and defined … that's what motivates my desire to suck all the cocks I can. I don't care about the rest of their bodies, their faces, their asses, much less having them do anything to me, to fuck me or suck me. They can fuck my mouth, but that's the end of the line for me. I'm a cocksucker and I don't want anything to interfere with that. A hundred percent of my attention is focused on pleasing the guy I'm sucking, giving him plea-sure with my tongue, my lips, my saliva and my breath, and sometimes also with my hands, sliding them along the shaft of his cock while my tongue plays with the head, or caressing his balls at the same time as I'm swallowing them whole.

I don't want anything from these guys other than that undeniable sign that I did a good job, and once I receive their offering of semen, I don't stay. I'm not seeking friends or camaraderie, not even from the guys I visit regularly. I only want one thing, and a lot of them love giving it to me.

Only once I'm back home do I let myself touch myself—my lips recreating their shape, the memory of their taste filling my mouth, the sound of them shouting as they come echoing in my memories—and I finally surrender control and give myself over to the orgasm and its unstoppable spasms and explosions.

NOIR

It was one of those evenings. I asked myself what I was doing in the office at that time of night, but I didn't have anywhere better to go. Even though anywhere would have been better than that room, with those two pieces of furniture: the old desk overflowing with the files of closed cases that were waiting to be sorted (a job I hate doing, which is why I let them pile up with the hope that they will either magically file themselves or I will be able to allow myself the luxury of hiring a secretary some day; I wasn't sure which of the two scenarios was more improbable) and the chair for clients, still empty after so long. I was about to leave and head to the gym (which is what I should do) or go get a drink (which is what I was more likely to do), when she came in, without knocking. I was surprised to see her; the truth is that not many women come up to my office.

She waited until I was looking at her and shot me a calculated smile.

It didn't have the effect she wanted. To hide that fact, I pointed her toward the chair. She crossed the office slowly, placing each slender leg in front of the other, seeking an effect that was just as calculated as her smile.

She was wasting her time, but I didn't care; I had time to lose.

She sat. I was waiting for her to tell me why she'd come to see me, but she only looked at me with that femme fatale smile, those bright red lips.

"What can I help you with?" I asked her, finally, in order to break the ice.

"It's my husband," she said.

I sighed. Same old story.

"I think he's cheating on me," she continued.

I wanted to send her packing. But I hadn't had a client in a long time, and I didn't need to check my bank balance to know that I shouldn't reject her at the first sign of trouble.

"Do you know who the other woman is?" I asked, opening a notebook to start taking notes.

"It's not a woman," she confessed. "I think they're men."

The case was beginning to sound much more interesting.

"What exactly is it that you want from me?"

"I want proof that my husband's gay. That's why I looked for a detective agency in a gay directory. I imagine you know the places where men like my husband do these things."

I nodded.

"Good," she said, and she relaxed, relieved at being able to hand her problem over to an appropriate professional. She opened her bag and took out a photograph, extending her arm to place the photo on the desk.

I looked at the snapshot. I'd fuck him right now, in front of her. Although it would be better for the agency's bottom line if it took me a few hours to gather the necessary proof. Maybe I wouldn't have to include all the details in my report.

I took a contract out of a drawer so she could sign it.

Things were looking up, both for the agency's bottom line and for my evening plans as well.

THE MULTIVERSE

There are philosophers who say that the world splits in two with every decision, like branching paths, and as a result there are millions and millions of parallel universes. I want to live in that other universe, the one where I kissed you instead of holding back out of fear it would destroy our friendship.

ADULT GAMES

Circling the sauna's dimly lit hallways, it struck me that we were adult men playing a game of hide and go seek. Except the rules were backwards and people would only hide, disappearing into a private booth, when two of them found each other. And sometimes, not even then. I leaned against an open doorway to watch how an encounter developed. And with my attention focused on how the guy who was already inside, sitting on the mattress, released from the folds of the towel the rigid dick of the guy who was standing up, and then brought it to his mouth, I was taken by surprise when the hand of the guy who was being sucked off touched me. I looked at him and he smiled at me, his hand slipping down to find my cock. He gave it a little tug, gentle but insistent, until I was also inside the booth. Ready or not, I was now part of the game.

DOWNLOADS

I opened the direct link to the videos of the day and, between sips of coffee, I began to decide which ones to download. Some were repeats, I could identify fragments of scenes I had already watched. That happened because certain clips or full movies would be uploaded more than once. But I didn't download them if I recognized them, unless my favorite actors appeared. Tim Kruger or Colby Keller. Dale Cooper or Rafael Alencar. I always download everything I find of theirs, even if I already have it. Just in case, so I don't miss anything. Even though the truth of the matter is I almost never go back and watch the videos once they're downloaded .... But I like having them. I like to know I can see them whenever I want. That's why I download everything I can every morning.

There are a lot of videos I reject right off the bat because they don't interest me. Like the ones about guys who are barely legal. But there are always a few videos left after I sort through them the first time, and then I have to decide whether I'm going to download them or not. I start opening them in new tabs and watch bits and pieces of each one ... enough to know whether they turn me on. And when the answer is yes, instead of watching more, I start downloading it because I know I want to have it and, in the meantime, I go to another tab and another video to see whether I like it. Because there are always so many to evaluate every morning, to know whether they're worth saving or not ...

The problem is that, with the excitement of watching enough to get to the real action, I end up finishing my own *download* before the movies are fully downloaded. That's why I never manage to watch any of the scenes in their entirety. After I come, I no longer have any desire to keep watching. I let the files keep downloading while I go shower and then I save them in a folder, which I transfer, every so often, to a hard drive where I save all the movies I've copied but haven't seen yet. I keep saving them, my erotic treasures, for some morning when I can't get online and I finally find the time to watch one of the scenes from start to finish.

IN THE STREET

We were coming up on Paseo del Prado when I raised my eyes and saw a guy who was watching me as he made his way down the cross street.

I returned his gaze and felt that moment of mutual recognition, but I wasn't sure if he was flirting with me or just also going to the Cuesta de Moyano to await the election results and, if luck was on our side (hopefully!), celebrate Manuela Carmena's victory as mayor.

We shared that energy, an ephemeral moment of connection, that was as powerful as it was fleeting: our eyes met, full of admiration or celebration or simply a glimmer of similarity. An ideological fling instead of a physical one. Or perhaps both things at the same time. I wasn't sure. And the truth of the matter is I didn't care.

I smiled at him and turned the corner and, together, we walked toward change.

BEHIND THE SCENES

We had one of those moments of total harmony that are so unusual that I wouldn't have been surprised to find out our breathing was synchronized. There's no question our pleasure was, him enjoying penetrating me slowly and as deep as possible and me enjoying his cock sliding in and out with every lunge. All of a sudden, I got a cramp in my right leg and my moans of pleasure turned into a long howl of pain.

Ricardo stopped immediately, right in the middle of a stroke, in case the pain was his fault, and looked at me with alarm and concern.

"It's not you," I gasped, contorting myself like a fish out of water to disconnect our bodies and be able to bend my leg at last. I was panting more now than during the intercourse, but for the wrong reasons.

"A cramp," I explained, when I gotten my breathing partially under control. I stretched my leg out completely, trying to get rid of that sudden and painful knot.

"Ouch," said Ricardo with sympathy, his face reflecting a mask of shared pain.

He began to caress the affected leg, massaging it with his big, warm hands.

"I'm sorry," I said, reaching out to grasp his dick, flaccid after that scare.

"No problem," he told me, and he bent over to kiss me, a long kiss, with tongue, before straightening up again and continuing to massage my leg. "I'm surprised it doesn't happen more often. Like in porn flicks. You see those dudes with their legs so wide apart, not because it's comfortable, but to give the cameras a better view of what's going on."

"I don't know ..." I answer. "Maybe it's because they're experts, or they really stretch out before they start filming, or they're not as old as I am ..."

His commentary had successfully distracted me from the pain, which had gotten less intense thanks to the attention from his hands; now it was more like the kinds of aches and pains we get after running or working out, somewhat uncomfortable, but perfectly manageable. I straightened my leg out again, like a dancer stretching, and then, smiling, I bent it a little, making an L shape that I used like a shepherd's crook to pull his body toward me. I smiled at him, changing position until we were lying side by side, and I told him: "How about we find a different position and try to start that scene back up where we left off?"

TREMORS

We were both on the sofa, me sprawled out with a detective novel and him sitting at the other end, playing around on his computer. He was wearing earphones so it wouldn't bother me while I was reading. I didn't know if he was watching a movie or listening to music. I couldn't see him unless I lowered my book, but I knew he was there, because from time to time, he would change positions and I could feel the vibrations down the length of the sofa. This was a usual thing for us and we didn't feel isolated even though we were each doing our own thing, our way of sharing domesticity.

Suddenly the sofa started moving a lot.

"Stop jumping around," I said, without taking my eyes off the page.

"It's not me," he answered, and then a beat later: "I think it's an earthquake."

That did make me lower my book and I raised my head to look around. Víctor was frozen in place, the computer still on his lap, but he'd taken off the headphones. He was sitting up, his body tense.

I could feel the sofa swaying.

"But the pictures on the wall aren't moving," I said.

"Yeah, but can you hear the bookcases?" he replied.

And he was right, a quiet sound was coming from them as they bumped into each other. The floor was wood and it wasn't completely flat.

It was so faint that I wouldn't have even realized it was an earthquake if it hadn't been for Víctor.

Suddenly, everything stopped and there was total calm with an unusual silence, except for the hum of music that was still coming out of his headset. Everything was motionless except for Víctor, who was still trembling, as if he were subject to the aftershocks of the earthquake, which never came.

I sat up and hugged him, whispering little nonsense phrases, while I cuddled him. After a while, he stopped trembling.

"I'm better now," he told me, smiling. "It reminded me of this earthquake in my town when I was little. We were right by the epicenter. But really, I'm fine."

He kissed me. Not a peck or a domestic kiss, but a real kiss, powerful, ardent, full of life and urgency and hunger.

His fear turned to passion, he needed to feel alive after being so scared.

We went to our bedroom and I focused on giving him pleasure, without letting him touch me or do anything to me, just enjoy it, until he was vibrating with pleasure through his whole body, provoking that eruption of white lava on his abdomen, and then I held him until those new tremors had also dissipated.

MARCOS

It wasn't being away from my own bed or the strange body next to mine that prevented me from falling asleep after fucking, but the *metronomic* tick tock of his pacemaker. He'd mentioned it to me before leaving the disco, after inviting me back to his place, so the scars on his chest wouldn't catch me unawares and so I had the opportunity to change my mind if I wanted. I'd never imagined such a young guy—21 years old— with something that we associate with old folks, but it didn't frighten me. It is true that when we got to his room in a shared flat, I was cautious at first, touching his body as if it were made of glass. I avoided touching his chest as I took off his clothes, until he grabbed my hands between his and pressed them against the scars—it was skin, marked by scars, but nothing more. I searched for his mouth with mine and we melted into a searing deep kiss, our bodies intertwined, the beat of the music from the disco playing in our ears again.

The sex was fun, and I was happy to accept when he asked if I wanted to spend the night, but I couldn't sleep yet, my body and brain alert to every sound, every movement, every thought. Now, in the calm after the storm, I wondered what his life must be like, while I listened to that rhythmic sound that reminded me of the crocodile from Peter Pan that swallowed a clock and chased after Captain Hook. I turned to try to sleep on my side, moving slowly so I wouldn't wake him. But he turned too, as if he were looking for me in his sleep, and his hand ended up resting on my butt.

I tried to count the ticks of his pacemaker, like counting sheep.

But I realized that the *tempo* was accelerating. For a minute, I was afraid something was wrong with him. But then just after that, I realized what must have happened, and with one hand, I reached behind me and found his dick, stiff and pulsating.

It seems Marcos couldn't sleep either.

COLD TURKEY

"You're not going to believe what I did this weekend," said Víctor, placing the tray with our coffees on the table and sitting down beside me.

I started to get a little bit excited, like Pavlov's dog. I rejected anything obviously extreme (an orgy with seven guys, a double penetration, etc.) because, even though for me, they only existed in porn and in my fantasies, for Víctor those types of things were his daily bread. We had one of those friendships that was forged in our youth that had survived the passing of time even though we had nothing in common. Except, perhaps, the fact that I'd been head over heels in love with him at one point, and he was also in love with himself .... We used to share an apartment in the Malasaña neighborhood with three other guys, but we'd lost contact with the rest of them a long time ago. Even though I was a few months older than him, Víctor had come to Madrid before I did, and he adopted me like his little brother, becoming my guide through the city, both during the day and at night, showing me the stores where I could buy secondhand clothes and the bars that served the cheapest drinks. And I masturbated night after night while listening to him fuck on the other side of the paper-thin wall that separated our bedrooms, imagining that I was the one in bed with him instead of that night's fling. But I never shared those fantasies with him, not back then, when we lived together, or now, when we got together for coffee every other Monday afternoon.

"I don't know," I said finally. "I give up. Tell me."

There was something comfortable about following our established roles: I was the faithful audience for his adventures.

"I deleted Grindr and Scruff from my phone."

He was right. I never would have guessed.

"What for?"

"So, the thing is, I was in bed with this guy, after we fucked, and he offered to let me spend the night, and I said yes, it had been fun and I thought we could fuck again in the morning, and I was enjoying it, like friends, nothing sappy. But I realized I was waiting for him to leave for a minute so I could look at the messages on my phone. So when he went to the bathroom, I deleted all my apps, without even reading them. Shock therapy. What do you think?"

I was dumbfounded. Had the time finally come to tell him? Or would it ruin everything?

"In a Hollywood movie, this would be the moment when you realize the perfect guy has been by your side the whole time."

Víctor laughed.

"Why haven't we ever fucked, you and me?" he said, serious again.

I couldn't answer. It wasn't for lack of desire on my part.

"I think there's a time after you know someone that if you still haven't fucked, it's never going to happen. In spite of what Hollywood tells us."

"Maybe."

"That's what I don't know how to handle right now. You're going to have to help me."

THE SAME RIVER

We left our shoes and socks on the riverbank to wade in almost up to our knees, the cool water relieving our feet and legs, which felt great after a morning of hiking.

"Do you know why you can't step into the same river twice?" he asked all of a sudden. "Because of the current. Even if the bed of the river you're in is the same, the water keeps moving and that's why it's a different river."

"Yeah, I get the idea."

"Well, I think it's the same with sex."

"What?"

"Even if you fuck the same person and you do all the same things, even in the same order, it would never be the same sex."

"I think you've got heatstroke. That's what happens when you don't wear a hat."

"Seriously. Think about it. Every time two people fuck it's different, even if they do it in the same place and same order. Because they're no longer the same people, they've got more experiences, including the previous times they had sex."

"This all sounds too Zen to me. But let's find some shade and put your theory to the test. That would be more fun than walking anymore."

"I think you mean than thinking so much," he said, splashing me with water before running to the shore and starting to pull off his clothes.

COUPLE SEX

I was on all fours while Bangs fucked me and I sucked Star. Obviously those were nicknames so I could distinguish who was who. Star because he had a tattoo of a star on his groin, which seemed to twinkle as I moved closer and then away from it, sliding my mouth along his cock. Bangs obviously because of his haircut, which was now dark from the sweat of our fucking.

They'd introduced themselves when I got to their apartment, but I don't know if they used their real names. I didn't give them mine. And since I wasn't planning on seeing them again, I didn't worry about trying to remember what they said. What I did want was to be able to distinguish them, and even though my sphincter noticed the difference between them, I needed to be able to identify which feeling belonged to each of them. That's why I gave them nicknames, which is one of the complications of anonymous sex with various people .... Although in this case, the stranger was me because they were a couple. Which was what I had looked for, to be a novelty for both of them and the focus of their attention.

There are people who like to live their fantasies within the security of their relationship. And others, like me, prefer to experience them anonymously. It's not because I'm a hypocrite, but some of my dreams are too raw to share with my partner. They're exciting precisely because they're what he doesn't give me and what I don't want to receive—at least not from him.

And that's why I found myself here, giving free rein to my kinkiest side with Bangs and Star, in spite of how unsexy their nicknames were. I could have baptized them Bratwurst and Beef Stick, but of course, I needed a way to distinguish them before I saw them naked, even if only in my own thoughts. But now I didn't want to think, just to feel. I loved being used by both of them, using my body to satisfy their own pleasure. They switched again, Bangs took off the condom and placed himself in front

129

of my mouth; I tried to swallow him whole while Star put on another condom. And then suddenly, I needed to suck air when Star rammed it all the way in. Moaning, I looked up and saw the two of them kissing above my body, each a witness and accomplice in sharing me.

KISSES

I bent my head toward him, but just before our lips touched, he turned.

"If you don't kiss, we're going to just give up on this," I told him.

I waited a moment, but even though he turned his head to look me in the eye, he didn't kiss me.

I pushed away his hand, which he had slipped under my towel to take hold of my dick, and asked him to leave. Leaning against the closed door, I hesitated between jacking off and going home or opening the door and waiting for another man. In the end, I opened the door. I couldn't kiss myself.

SYMPHONY

I wake up first and look at you, still asleep, by my side. The sheets have slipped off but they're still wrapped around your body, covering and revealing different bits of skin.

I know that if I reach out to touch you, your skin will still preserve the warmth of sleep. I also know that, with a single finger, I can bring you pleasure, excite you until you wake up from an overdose of pleasure.

I've never understood why, for so many men, the image of a dick or an ass that they haven't touched/sucked/fucked can excite them so much, often more than the person they have by their side.

I'm all nerves the first time I'm intimate with someone, I can't relax enough to enjoy myself, so I try to make the other guy enjoy it to the max. But there're still so many uncertainties: what he does and doesn't like, how he's going to react, if there's chemistry between us ... things we can only discover in the act, by taking the plunge.

For me, the magic resides in knowing how he's going to respond to my touch, my mouth, my dick, the things we can each do to make one another feel pleasure, like a musician, practicing and practicing, until you disappear into the music, the parts coming together to form a whole that's perfect and bigger than any individual piece.

Looking at you as you sleep, running my eyes over your naked body beneath the sheet, my dick rises like a director's baton, ready for the symphony to begin.

CALCULATED RISK

Sitting naked on the edge of the tub, I unscrewed the head of the shower hose, replacing it with a thin metal tube. I'd been lucky that this apartment had such an old-fashioned bathroom; in my previous one, which I also shared, the shower was super modern, with jets of water all over the place and rain that fell from above. Very relaxing, but not at all practical for me. I turned on the faucet until the water had warmed to a pleasant temperature and turned it off again. I already had the bottle of Eros open on the edge of the sink, and I squeezed a couple of drops of lubricant onto the tube. As I spread the gel along the length of its warm surface, it looked like I was giving the tube a hand job and my dick started to get hard out of empathy, but my body wasn't just asking me to beat off. That's why I was doing so much prep work before going out partying. Inhaling deeply, I stuck the lubricated tube up my ass and turned the faucet back on slowly. It was a curious sensation of warmth and fullness.

Just then, the door to the bathroom opened. I thought I was the only one home and hadn't bolted the door.

"Sorry, I didn't know there was anyone in here," said Dioni, before looking at the scene again. "What the fuck are you doing?"

I turned the water off and answered: "Getting ready to go out."

"Do you have a date? Or is this all just in case?"

"Just in case," I confessed.

"Hmm," he said, and he looked at me for an extended beat before adding: "It seems like a lot of effort for such a low guarantee of return on investment. But have fun. If you don't have any luck, I'm not going out today. If you see the light on under my door when you get back, go ahead and knock."

He left, closing the door behind him. I still wasn't sure if he came in because he needed to take a piss, or just to wash his hands, or what. I pulled out the tube, clenching tight to keep the liquid inside. I replaced the head on the shower hose so my flatmates could use it. My thoughts were going a thousand miles a minute, doing the math. It was obvious that he had hit on me, but in a manner that was so ... offhanded.

I was vacillating between going out as I had planned, with the possibility of not scoring, as had happened so many times in the past, or taking advantage of Dioni's offer. But what if it didn't work?

They always say you shouldn't soil your own nest.

I sat on the toilet and finally released everything I had inside. Whatever I decided, I thought, we'll all enjoy it more now. I took a quick shower and dried off. I went out into the hallway, wearing just the towel. I stopped in front of Dioni's room, looking at the ray of light that was visible underneath it. I had reached the crux of the dilemma: get dressed or knock on his door.

BELONGING

I learned to get rid of my jealousy by drinking yerba mate in Argentina.

At first, when cradling the warm gourd in my hand, I didn't want to drink out of the bombilla, that metal straw that everyone had used before me. As a newcomer to Buenos Aires, it struck me as unhygienic. But I didn't have any choice if I wanted to fit in, and that's what I wanted; I'd come to stay. I closed my eyes and took a sip, almost burning my tongue with the hot, bitter liquid. I later learned it can be sweetened, but by then, I was used to the flavor. And little by little, I found my place in the city.

And also in a group of friends.

We organized private parties, at one person's house or another.

And of course, I like some of them more than others. But I've discovered that what I like best is belonging to the group, how we share something communal.

So I don't feel jealous or impatient anymore; I know my turn will come.

And when one of them gets up off the couch and stops right in front of me, I cup my hands and caress his scrotum as if it were a yerba mate gourd, warm beneath my fingers.

And I don't think about what mouths have touched that bombilla before me, I just bow my head.

And then I say gracias.

And I pass him on.

TOO BIG, TOO SMALL

Very large cocks are awe-inspiring, they can inspire envy, or even the desire to touch them, to possess them, but the truth is they're not very practical. They don't fit everywhere, no matter how hard we try to swallow them whole. Sometimes they serve as challenges, like those who train to climb Mount Everest: we dilate with butt plugs and poppers, we use silicone lubricants or new gels, we find XL condoms, but even then, there are some that are so big they defeat us. Or when we're finally ready, their owners can't quite stay hard, and we wait with our legs spread wide while they beat off enough to wake it up and fill it with enough blood so we can both enjoy ourselves .... In my experience, big dicks are impressive, and very pretty to see and touch, but for fucking, I prefer dicks that are more manageable. But not too tiny either .... Better a cock that's thick even though it's short than a long one that's too thin. For sure, the ideal is: a little more than what fits in my mouth so I can make an effort and manage to swallow that extra centimeter ... For me, that dick, as Goldilocks would say, is just right.

THE MORNING AFTER

Waking up at someone else's place always means getting up on the wrong side of the bed for me. Sometimes literally, like today, when I kicked a wall that shouldn't have been there ... and I realized I wasn't in my own bed. Still groggy from the lack of caffeine and sleep, I didn't remember where I was or who I'd gone to bed with. I didn't want to open my eyes yet and dispel all the possibilities with harsh reality. I wanted to continue fantasizing.

I'd gone to a Eurovision party at my friend Peio's place. It was a very international party, with very handsome men from lots of different countries. I spent more time admiring what was on offer in the live show than paying attention to the screen with all those generic songs, almost all sung in English, which made it harder for me to remember what country they were all from .... It was more interesting to let everyone else yell or criticize the outfit of one contestant or the voice of another, while I reviewed geography lessons with the bodies in my field of vision.

Liam was very easy to remember, a prototypical Irish lad, lanky and shy with a red beard. We all asked for his hand, jokingly, to celebrate the referendum that allowed same-sex marriage in Ireland. But all of us would have really liked to go to bed with him, especially Pierre, a French guy who clung to Liam like a remora all night long. A shame, but there were a lot of other fish in the sea ... and other guys at the party.

Kostas from Athens, for example. Without opening my eyes, I licked my lips, trying to feel if they were irritated from making out for hours, from rubbing them against his bearded chin, his hairy chest ... but no, they were dry, but nothing more than that. In fact, I might have started questioning whether I'd used them at all last night, for kissing or for sucking or for anything else, if it weren't for the fact of waking up naked in an unknown bed. That would have been typical for me, and also typical of how the night had gone, with very tight voting between the

Swedish singer, who was very cute but a homophobe, and Russia ... which was worse.

Maybe I hadn't gotten lucky with any of the foreigners, not Carsten from Austria, or Gerard from Belgium, or Urban from Slovenia, but with one of the other Spaniards. With my luck, it would be Raúl. We'd already hooked up a few times, when there wasn't anyone better around, and ... the sex was so insipid that it would have been better to go back home alone and take care of things myself.

My foot began to burn with the pain of kicking the wall. It was time to open my eyes and confront reality. And today was election day! I had to go vote.

"Want coffee?" a voice asked me in English, interrupting my mental catalog of catastrophes. And I smiled, before opening my eyes and seeing Liam with a coffee mug in his hand.

Maybe my luck had changed and there actually was hope for the future.

SLEEPING BEAUTY

Even while still asleep, its splendor could be intuited.

I caressed it, but it didn't respond.

I kissed it, but still nothing.

"I'm sorry," he said, "but after doing all those lines ..."

But I didn't want to accept defeat so easily.

I placed it in my mouth and began to suck. The magic of my mouth worked, and the story finally came to its happy ending.

RETURNING HOME

For me, the sexiest part of traveling is returning home.

It's not that I don't enjoy seeing new and different men, their beautiful, exotic bodies. And I confess that I'm sometimes tempted. But I have a closed relationship and one of the things I love about it is how well we know each other. Sex with someone you know so well is very different from sex with a stranger, someone who doesn't know what really gets you going. Someone with whom the sex, even if it's pleasurable, is meaningless in the sense of being ephemeral, remaining on a physical and animal level.

Returning home, especially after I've been in the States, is also an ideal time for us, given my jet lag.

My boyfriend likes morning sex. He wakes up with a hard-on and the desire to use it.

Me, on the other hand, I'm an ogre in the morning. One of those people who can't talk until they've had their first cup of coffee; and I don't drink coffee, so just imagine how unpleasant I am.

I prefer to make love and then fall asleep, because after coming, I collapse into a vegetative state.

So we're normally a bit off kilter when it comes to the desire to fuck. Our compromise is to screw at lunchtime. So then afterwards, I can take a nap and he can go work in his office, invigorated by our sexual activity.

But the best times are when I get back from a transatlantic trip: me still awake from the time change and him just waking up and raring to go like always ...

Just thinking about what I can expect when I get home makes me hard as I wait for my bags to appear. Adjusting my trousers, I feel like a teenager again, with my over-stimulated hormones.

Ah, the anticipation ...

I know people who swear that make-up sex after a fight is the hottest. But if I've been in an argument, I'm still analyzing what the other person said, what I could have said, and I don't feel like fucking.

But I-missed-you sex is fantastic.

The waiting. The desire.

It's like waiting for your bags. You see a lot that are the same size and color as yours but they're not it. Then there's that moment of hope and relief when you think it's come out ... but no, it's someone else's. Until finally, it arrives, and you feel elated; with a smile on your face, you walk toward customs, fearing that your expression will make them think they should inspect your belongings. In the end, you get through without any problem. You're almost home now.

In the taxi, I send him a text with one hand while repositioning my erection with the other. Won't be long now ...

NEW TECHNOLOGY

A decade ago, he would have asked for the guy's phone number or given his own. But the group said goodbye before there was an opportunity for that old-fashioned ritual. Once he was alone, he took out his phone and opened Grindr, hoping the other guy had done the same. Just in case, he opened the rest of them: Scruff, GROWLr, PlanetRomeo, Tinder. It was the modern version of cruising: walking past someone on the street and then turning and looking back over your shoulder; or now, both opening a hook-up app and searching for one another. But he didn't show up. Even though he stayed there, waiting, leaning against a doorway, not wanting to move too far away so he would still be locatable by GPS. Finally, he returned home, sad but not resigned. He logged onto Facebook to look for him among the friends of the acquaintances they had in common, but he didn't find him. He must use a nickname, because he didn't show up with the name he had given him. So he scrolled through all the profile pictures, but still without success. All the new technology had failed him. He jacked off and finally went to bed.

The next day, between the lack of sleep and his frustrated search the previous night, the whole world looked gray to him. He was in a bad mood when he got to work. Until, during a break, he recognized the guy from the previous night among his new followers on Instagram. The day suddenly lit up, as if someone had added a bright new filter to it.

LOVE IS IN THE HAIR

When I was six or seven years old, my friend Martín and I kidnapped a couple of my sister's dolls. As part of the torture of the captives, we took off all their clothes. That was the primary objective of our game, even though neither of us would have admitted it. I think that, at that age, we didn't even know it ourselves. But I still remember the disappointment I felt when we took off their pants, both the girl's and the guy's, and discovered that they didn't have anything more than a hairless bulge. I'd seen adult men naked, and I knew they had dark hair there, between their legs, in addition to soft parts hanging down, not like ours (which we had compared, of course), which were still small and hard. I felt proud when my hair started to grow in, and I didn't understand the guys who take it all off. Nowadays, every time I'm with a guy and I pull off his underwear and find out he shaves, I feel that childhood disappointment all over again. I like real men, the hairier the better!

That's why I realized I was really into Efrén when one day, after we'd had sex, he offered to shave my pubes for me and I didn't kick him out of my bed or my life.

"But, what for?"

He stuck two fingers in his mouth and pulled out a hair.

"So? We're men! We should be hairy!"

"Do it for me."

And since I was just a bit crazy for him, I did it.

The process was worse than I'd imagined. First, we shaved the area with an electric razor. Every movement caused an unsettling breeze.

"Can't we leave it like that?" I begged.

Efrén took out a disposable razor and shaving cream. My balls contracted in fear, and we had to stretch the skin out by hand to shave them completely. And of course, if Efrén was helping me, it got me excited, which only prolonged the agony.

Exhausted and feeling like a plucked chicken, I collapsed on the bed, with my hands protecting my genitals, as if I could cover them until the hair grew back.

Efrén climbed on top of me and tried to kiss me, but I kept my lips closed. So he started kissing my body, moving down, burrowing into the hair on my chest, tickling my nipples with his tongue …. He kissed my ribs and circled my belly button with his tongue, before following that path that led from the belly button down to where I used to have a bush framing my dick and balls. He forced my hands away, and I had to resist the urge to cross my legs and protect myself, when he lowered his head and I felt his breath on my naked skin.

And suddenly his tongue, warm and damp, pressed against the skin of my ball sack, and a single-voweled moan slipped out of me: "Ooooooooooooo," and I finally understood why guys shave down there.

OBSERVATIONS

The party had already begun when I got there. A man, naked except for a jockstrap and sneakers, opened the door and handed me a plastic bag. I took off all my clothes, right there in the dimly lit entranceway, and put them into the bag, just leaving my shoes and socks on (although I soon found out that a lot of people had taken them off as well). The jockstrap guy clipped a clothespin with a number onto the bag and gave me an elastic bracelet with that same number printed on its plastic token. Then he took me down the hallway to show me everything. The apartment had several rooms, each one filled by groups of guys in every possible combination. Latex sheets covered the couches and there were inflatable mattresses on the floors. I went into the bathroom to pee, partially out of nerves and to empty my bladder in a preventive fashion, and in part (I admitted to myself) to delay the moment when I had to decide what to do. I went back down the hallway, feeling like I was in a huge sex circus trying to observe the action in all three tents at the same time. On the left, I watched a guy kneeling on all fours on one of the mattresses, sucking one guy's dick while another man fucked him in the ass. On my right, there were three guys sitting on the sofa, encouraging a fourth who was sucking them off in turn one right after the other. All of a sudden, I felt a hand on my hip, so I looked straight in front of me and then lowered my gaze. A man was crouched before me, his mouth open, his eyes asking for permission. I was still only half hard, excited by what I was seeing but still distant. The time had come to stop being an observer. I nodded my head and the guy smiled at me, before turning his attention to my dick. He lifted it in one hand, weighing it in his palm as it started to grow under his admiring gaze. He kissed the tip and then moved his tongue in circles between the foreskin and the head. I closed my eyes to concentrate on the sensation of sinking into the depths of the hot dampness of his mouth. When I opened them again, my eyes met those of a guy lying on his back on the sofa with his legs spread wide: he smiled at me and gave me a thumbs up before returning his attention to the guy who was fucking him. I realized that now I was the one framed by the doorway and that, by starting to participate in the action of the party with the guy who was sucking me off, I had shifted from observer to observable.

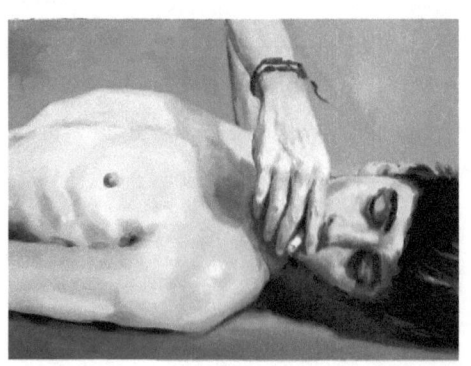

PHONE CALL

"Don't stop," I tell you when the phone rings. "It's sure to be your mom."

She always calls when we're fucking. Even though we let the machine pick up, we've lost our rhythm, your thrusts now synchronized with the ringing of the phone.

It's taking ages for both of us to come.

"Should we give up?"

You say no with your head and a renewed surge of energy as you fuck me.

Afterwards, I light a cigarette and try to hand it to you. But you don't even wait long enough to take a drag, getting out of bed, looking for the handset.

SHARED EXPERIENCES

After the protest in front of the Partido Político headquarters, Ximo and I went to the Eagle to have a beer and catch up. Even though he was staying at my place, he had arranged to meet up with other friends for dinner later on and they would probably go out clubbing. Our friendship was based on so many shared experiences that he was now more like family than my real one. Some of our acquaintances wondered whether we were or had been lovers, they said we acted like an old married couple. But the truth is that nothing had ever happened between us, even though we often went out in search of sex together. We'd been together during sexual encounters, but we'd never done it together, not directly. We were too similar, not so much physically, but in our tastes. If we'd lived in the same city, we'd probably have had more conflicts, but neither of us was possessive, not in sex, nor in activism (where we were more interested in results than in having a starring role). Maybe that's why our friendship lasted.

We drank our beers leaning against the wall, having a post-mortem on the protest and discussing how to keep this momentum going. It didn't strike either of us as weird to be talking about these things while we watched as a customer gave the bartender head or a nearby screen showing a fist fucking scene. Both the sex and the activism were an integral part of our lives, just like our interest in good food and culture.

"There's an exhibition of French sculptures at the MAPFRE Foundation that I want to see," Ximo commented. He could keep our conversation going, but I knew him and it was clear that his attention was focused on some guy.

"I haven't seen it yet," I told him, looking around to see who had captured his interest. "We can go tomorrow morning before you catch the train."

I saw him too, and for a moment, we both inhabited a silence full of shared admiration. There are a lot of men at the gym with sculpted bodies that seem more like polystyrene than muscle. But this guy's body was large, virile, a gift of nature more than of narcissistic exercise.

Ximo has always been more daring than I am, and he disappeared from my side to go over to him. They talked for a while, and then Ximo knelt down and started to blow him right there. It wasn't out of exhibitionism as much as urgency, and I couldn't help but watch. Other people approached the two of them, blocking my view, but then I realized Ximo was blowing someone else. The first guy stayed there, still erect, watching the action that had moved to another place. I approached him and knelt down in front of him, thinking we'd never been so close, Ximo and me, while my saliva mixed with his on this stranger's hard cock.

JUST WHAT I ORDERED

The maître d' sat us at a table next to the window.

"This is great," you joked once we were seated. "They'll give us bigger portions to seduce everyone who's walking by."

The waiter appeared at our table. I looked up from the menu and felt an electric current: of recognition, of desire. We'd seen each other before, although always at the wrong place or time.

You didn't realize.

"Sweetie," you said, staking a claim without knowing it. "Do you want to share the *Gambas Diavolo*?"

I looked at the waiter as I answered you: "Whatever you want."

He smiled at me.

When we finished eating, you asked for the check.

"My treat," I said, putting my hand on the bill and feeling somewhat guilty. "To celebrate ... just for the hell of it."

You smiled at me, and I smiled back.

But I kept thinking about that other smile, that other mouth.

I had enough cash, but I used a credit card: a way of telling him my name, at least.

Before I folded the bill and stuck it in my wallet, I saw there was something written on the back: a phone number and a name.

Out on the street, holding your hand, I looked over my shoulder at our table in the window.

The waiter was clearing it. He was watching me, and when he saw I was looking at him too, he smiled.

THEN AND NOW

Back then, it was possible to have a one-night stand. Have a good time and be done with it. If he slept over, you gave him a coffee in the morning before shooing him out. But it didn't involve anything else.

But now, between cell phones and e-mails, messages on the websites or apps where we meet one another, any hook up turns into a relationship.

And this innovation has me yelling at the screen, like some straight dude shouting at the TV during a soccer match: "I had a good time. But the fact that we've fucked doesn't mean you have to friend me on Facebook. Enjoy the good memories, like a summer fling, but that's as far as it goes. Stop insisting."

Because I'm too polite to reply in writing and tell him to fuck off. And because any reply means solidifying and recognizing a relationship beyond what it was: one night together that was nice until his cyberstalking (he must have read my last name on the doorbell downstairs) left me with this sour taste in my mouth.

GUILT

I don't know what makes me feel guiltier: taking your towel off the hook in the bathroom and throwing it in the dirty clothes basket or sleeping with one of your friends. I didn't recognize him at first, nor him me. But when he mentioned you—not by name, but in an anecdote I remembered—that's when I realized why he seemed familiar. You introduced us a few weeks ago in Bar Atril. In reality, he's not your friend, strictly speaking, but the best friend of your friend. I almost didn't fuck him, knowing you would find out, sooner or later. But anyway. Whatever it is that we have, it seems like sex isn't the driving force. At least between us. And it's not like the sex with him was anything out of this world. But I was tired of waiting for you. And of feeling guilty for waiting for you.

WRITERS BLOCK

I got there first, so I looked for a free table that was big enough for all of us. Since the life of a writer is so solitary, we'd formed an informal group to have a drink every week, a type of mutual support (or, really, encouragement) society.

Everyone else started to show up, until the last to arrive, Enrique, got his drink and sat down with us at the last free chair at the table.

"You don't look very happy," I said. "What's up, you haven't been making much progress this week?"

"Not at all!" he responded. "I'm still on the same scene."

"What's it about?" asked Julia. "Maybe we can help you get through it."

"It's a love scene between Sergio and Sebas ..."

We almost all started to groan.

"Sex scenes are the worst to write ..." said Paco.

"That's as true as true can be," agreed María. "They're a nightmare."

"I always question every word," said Julia. "I can't tell whether I've crossed the line between writing something literary and writing porn ..."

"The thing is," Enrique confessed, "I'm not really having a hard time writing it. The problem is that when I start describing the scene in question, I get too excited ... and then I have to stop and masturbate."

"Now I'm intrigued," said María. "What happens in the scene?"

"And... can't you go back to writing after you shoot your load?" asked Paco.

"The problem ..." Enrique began, "is that I'm one of those guys who falls asleep after coming. So every time I jack off, I have to take a nap."

"Just like my boyfriend," said María. "It doesn't matter if we fuck in the morning or at night, he always crashes afterwards."

"In that case, I hope you finish before he does," said Julia, and we all laughed.

"The worst part of it," confessed Enrique "is that I'm too old to be beating off three time a day! Every day! I'm starting to hate sitting down at the computer. And Marcos is mad because I no longer have the energy or the inclination to do anything when we see each other."

"You need to finish that chapter, or it's going to be the end of your relationship," said Julia.

"I'm still curious about what happens in the scene," insisted María. "Can you bring it next week?"

"But printed," added Paco. "Not to read out loud."

"Why? Are you afraid it'll make you too horny when you hear it?" asked Julia.

"Or that it'll turn poor Enrique on when he has to read it," I said.

"When the book's published, it should have a warning label: not appropriate for heterosexuals."

INDIVISIBLE PACK

As we were out walking off our supper, we saw a blond guy coming toward us down Las Ramblas. We looked at each other for a moment, and without a word, it was all decided. It had been a long time since we found a guy we were both into. Longer yet since we'd managed to hook up on the street. It must have been that Stefan, as a foreigner, still remembered those old traditions of hooking up live and not always through the phone or computer. Or maybe he was just horny, and that's why it didn't shock him when we invited him home.

We offered him something to drink and he accepted a glass of water, but he only wet his lips before setting it on a coaster on the coffee table like the perfect guest. And then, with perfect equanimity, he extended both arms so he could touch the two of us at the same time. And we looked at each other again, just a second, before focusing our attention on him, certain now that we were all going to enjoy the night. With that gesture, Stefan showed us that he had experience in sex with couples, that he had joined us for a real three-way. Sometimes we've invited guys home, but they end up clinging to one of us, without realizing that we're an indivisible pack. We're not interested in sharing our bed with other guys because we're bored as a couple or because we need to rekindle the spark, but because there are things we can do with three or four bodies that are impossible with just two.

That night, without rushing, we ended up in bed, us and Stefan, reveling in the possibilities, all of us enjoying together.

HYPERBOLE

If one were to believe everything he read on the hookup sites, normal men have been replaced by a type of superior homosexual race. The Hyper Homosexuals?

The protagonist of every profile is worthy of appearing in *The Guinness Book of World Records*.

None of them just likes to be fucked, they're always insatiable, mega-bottoms ... black holes into which anything or any person could disappear.

No one likes to simply penetrate, they're all power tops, studs, jackhammers ... virile members divorced from their bodies.

You don't hook up with a person but with a tourist brochure. And anyone who's ever gone on vacation knows that the photos in the flyer don't have much to do with reality when we actually reach the destination ...

How does one find domesticity, everyday affection?

Maybe I'm going to the wrong sites, and there are others I haven't yet discovered, where all the hyperbole is about intimacy and caring.

A hug already seems almost hyperbolic, it's only one e away from huge.

If anyone knows a page like that, please send me the URL.

THE SOUNDS OF NATURE

"What a pleasure to get out of the city!" I said, stretched out next to the stream. "Every time I come to a place like this, I wonder how I can go back to the city. Of course, when we're there, we get trapped by the routine and it's hard to get away again ... But listen to the incredible sounds of nature. The water from the river, the song of the birds ..."

Juan stuck his hand under the waistband of my shorts.

"What are you doing? I'm in the middle of a sublime and philosophical moment here, and you respond like you've got a one-track mind."

"You told me to listen to the sounds of nature."

"Exactly."

"Well, what do you think all those sounds mean? The singing of the birds, the croaking of the frogs. They want to fuck. The reason the flowers are so pretty is to seduce the bee so it'll take their pollen to another flower."

I couldn't say anything because he was right. Even though I didn't want to admit it.

After a long silence, I took his hand, and this time, I was the one who stuck it under the waistband of my shorts.

Juan smiled at me.

"OK, now listen to another sound of nature," he told me. "I want you to fuck me."

URGENCY

The secret of hooking up on the streets is to look not for beauty but thirst. Only if shared can hunger sate desire.

TRANSLATOR'S NOTE

by Sandra Kingery

Lawrence Schimel, a native New Yorker but long-time resident of Madrid, is a prolific writer and translator, but *A Beard Paradox* is the first of his fiction for adults that he wrote in Spanish, his "step-mother tongue." The 100 short pieces that comprise *A Beard Paradox* are TikTok-sized vignettes representing a mosaic of gay male experience in the age of Grindr. One of my challenges as the translator of these stories was to maintain the directness of the eroticized language, while also capturing the humor, warmth, and passion of the original. Spanish has a nice earthy relationship with body parts and sexual acts, where English sexual vocabulary often seems to straddle the extremes of down-and-dirty or mechanical. I wanted to make sure that the stories in English did not feel either more crude or more clinical than they were in the original.

Translating this book was one of the most enjoyable projects I have undertaken, but had I listened to a number of my colleagues, I might not have accepted the challenge. While one might assume that my colleagues' concern was related to the subject matter, that's not actually the case. Some of my translator friends questioned the wisdom of translating a book by an award-winning translator, particularly since I would be translating into his own native language. In spite of their concern, my experience in working with Lawrence was quite the opposite. It was very helpful and enjoyable to work with an author who fully understands and appreciates the translator's task, and every suggestion that Lawrence made about my translation helped to make it stronger.

I was also challenged by a well-established translator who questioned why I was translating this book rather than a text by a woman, the implication being that feminist translators should spend our time giving voice to underrepresented female authors. While I'm delighted to contemplate the idea that one might think we are at a place where gay male erotica is too mainstream to need to be championed, I believe our literary tradition is enriched by any text that reminds us that love is love and that human desire in all its variations is complex and important and challenging and profound. This particular collection fulfills those goals with much more joy and humor and unabashed pleasure than most. It was my honor to have the opportunity to translate it.

ACKNOWLEDGMENTS

Author & translator give thanks to the editors of the following publications where some of these stories were first published in English, sometimes in earlier drafts:

The Barcelona Review: Balcony Fishing, Death in Ibiza, Home Visit, Location, Outdoor Café, Puppy Love, Shared Codes
Erato: Fresh Sheets, Hot Line, Writing Exercise
Hawaii Review: Connection, Fresh from the Oven, Marked Territory, Nostalgia, Overheard, Porn Sequence
Image OutWrite: Calculations
Litro Magazine: Barista, Cat Sitter, Fresh Sheets, Lost Cat, Microverse, Writing Exercise
Moon Park Review: Hot Line
Peculiar: Le petite mort
Queen Mob's: A Beard for Two, Hot and Cold, Lunch Time
Río Grande Review: Afterwards, Precariousness
Words Without Borders: Grafted, Machos in the Metro, Pride